Emer O'Sullivan, * 1957, aufgewachsen in Dublin, hat dort und in Berlin Germanistik und Anglistik studiert. Sie war Stipendiatin für Kinder- und Jugendliteratur der Berliner Stiftung Preußische Seehandlung und arbeitet jetzt am Institut für Jugendbuchforschung der Johann Wolfgang Goethe-Universität in Frankfurt a. M.

Dietmar Rösler, * 1951, aufgewachsen in Emden, Studium in Berlin. Zwischen 1977 und 1996 Arbeit an den Fachbereichen Germanistik des University College Dublin, der Freien Universität Berlin und des King's College London. Seither Professor für Deutsch als Fremdsprache an der Universität Gießen.

Bei rotfuchs gibt es außerdem:
«I like you – und du?» (Band 20323), «It could be worse – oder?» (Band 20374), «Butler & Graf» (Band 20480), «Butler, Graf & Friends: Nur ein Spiel?» (Band 20531) und «Butler, Graf & Friends: Umwege» (Band 20647).

Emer O'Sullivan / Dietmar Rösler

Mensch, be careful!

Eine deutsch-englische
Geschichte

Rowohlt Taschenbuch Verlag

16. Auflage August 2005

Originalausgabe
Veröffentlicht im Rowohlt Taschenbuch Verlag,
Reinbek bei Hamburg, Mai 1986
Copyright © 1986 by Rowohlt Taschenbuch Verlag GmbH,
Reinbek bei Hamburg
Umschlaggestaltung any.way, Barbara Hanke
(Umschlagfoto: Per Koopmann)
Gesetzt aus der Garamond (Linotron 202)
Gesamtherstellung Clausen & Bosse, Leck
Printed in Germany
ISBN 3 499 20417 7

Inhaltsverzeichnis

Der Zusammenprall

Bored. Absolutely bored stiff, she was. That bloody boat had just left on time. She had only been five minutes late. Typical. These Germans, always did everything on time. And the words they had which never ended. *Hafenrundfahrtsboot!* What a name. Fiona kicked a stone into the water. Oh God, what a boring Sunday.

Das Fliegengitter war aufgeschnitten. Das fiel Edzard als Erstes auf. Und das Fenster stand offen, war nicht bloß aufgeklappt wie sonst immer. Edzard fuhr fast jeden Sonntag am Gebäude der *Friesland Fisch* vorbei. Er mochte den Fischgeruch. Das mit dem Fenster ließ ihn stutzen. Sonntags luden zwar manchmal die Arbeiter Waren in den Tiefkühl-LKW, aber sonst war hier nie was los. Doch ein offenes Fenster und keine Leute? Edzard lehnte das Fahrrad an die Hauswand und beschloss, sich die Sache etwas näher anzusehen.

So what! Who needs boats anyway, Fiona thought. I can cycle out to the sea just as well. She rode along the narrow footpath next to the Delft, as this part of the Emden harbour was called. Families were on their Sunday afternoon walks; on the other side of the Delft the big red ship, the *Deutsche Bucht*, commanded everybody's attention. As she was looking at it, too, Fiona nearly knocked down a middle-aged man walking his dog.

«Pass doch auf, das ist kein Fahrradweg!», the man roared at her. Grrrr, Fiona said to herself. What am I doing in this place? Why the hell did I come here at all? After passing through a lovely arch, the one that was on lots of picture postcards of Emden, she found herself on a wide area covered with cobblestones. Clatter clatter. Her bicycle shook and rattled and her teeth knocked together. There was no wall or any kind of barrier between the cobblestones and the water. It must be fantastic to cycle full blast into the water from here, she thought. Gather up speed, head for the edge and whee! She imagined flying through the air before crash-landing in the water. At least that would bring a bit of excitement into these boring old holidays.

Drinnen stand eine Maschine, die wohl zum Verpacken der Heringe benutzt wurde. Sonst nichts. Nichts? Ganz eindeutig war da ein Geräusch. Edzard wusste nicht genau, wonach es sich anhörte. Er überlegte einen Moment, schaute nach links und rechts, sah niemanden und glitt in den Raum. Er blickte um sich. Der Raum war zur Hälfte gekachelt, links eine Tür. Verschlossen. An der Wand gegenüber eine Waage und eine Art Fließband. Plötzlich ein neues Geräusch. Ein Rumpeln und dann so, als ob jemand Wasser ausgoss. Edzard zuckte zusammen. Es kam von rechts. Vorsichtig ging er dem Geräusch nach. Sieben, acht Schritte, dann kam er zu einem nur schwach durchsichtigen Vorhang; lauter schwere, schmutzige Plastikstreifen hingen von der Decke herunter. Hinter dem Vorhang schimmerte etwas Orangenes. Edzard schob zwei Plastikstreifen ein wenig auseinander.

Das Orangene vor ihm war ein Gabelstapler. Er drückte sich an die linke Wand, schob den Vorhang zur Seite und lugte um die Ecke. Ein hoher Stapel leerer Öldosen versperrte ihm die Sicht. Langsam und leise schob er sich durch den Vorhang und versteckte sich hinter den Dosen. Im Augenblick war es ganz still. Vorsichtig spähte Edzard um die Ecke. Am hinteren Ende der Halle, mit dem Rücken zu ihm, stand ein Mann, elegant gekleidet, in einer Lache aus Blut und Wasser. Auf dem Boden verstreut massenweise tote Fische.

In the distance Fiona saw some huge cranes. Cycling on, she passed a sign saying:

Hafengebiet. Keine öffentliche Straße. Das Befahren ist Unbefugten verboten. Nur für Fahrzeuge zur Be- und Entladung auf eigene Gefahr. Für Schäden jeglicher Art wird nicht gehaftet.

Wasser- und Schifffahrtsamt Emden

Unbefugten, Fiona read. *Unfug,* that meant something like nonsense. At least that's what she remembered from school. *Nicht gehaftet! Haft* was something like having to go to prison. If you do any nonsense in the harbour area you don't have to go to prison, she translated to herself. Funny crowd, these Krauts, printing something like that here, she thought, and cycled on.

Edzard wusste nicht, ob er lachen sollte oder nicht. Der Typ und die toten Fische, die passten überhaupt nicht zusammen. Sieben große grüne Fässer lagen geöffnet und umgestürzt auf dem Boden. Ein Irrer, das konnte nur ein Irrer sein. Dahinten in der Halle waren noch massenweise Fässer aufgestapelt. Ob er die auch noch alle umkippen wollte? Der Mann hatte inzwischen begonnen, mit einem anderen Gabelstapler eine neue Palette mit Fässern herunterzuholen. Aha, der Gabelstapler, das war also das Geräusch gewesen. Die blauen Fässer stellte der Mann achtlos zur Seite, die wenigen grünen machte er auf, fuhr mit der Hand in sie hinein und kippte sie dann um. Ein systematischer Irrer, dachte Edzard. Fast hätte er laut gelacht.

Fiona rode along a narrow pathway, water on one side, a run-down old building on the other. Bits of wood, planks were lying around with some small heaps of corn strewn between. It looked pretty deserted. Old concrete slabs were standing by the edge of the water. On the right wooden shutters, half-open, were swinging from a red-bricked wall. She got off her bicycle and looked in behind them. Trees, bushes, sacks of rubbish, old iron, rope, a broken ladder. And the place smelt a bit funny. She was only a few minutes away from all the walkers and their children in their Sunday best, but the place felt very strange and spooky.

Der Mann war offensichtlich wütend, er schimpfte vor sich hin, aber Edzard verstand nicht viel. Bloody hell oder so meinte er herausgehört zu haben. Vielleicht ein Engländer? War da gestern nicht was in den Nachrichten, Fischereikrieg in der EG oder so? Der Mann stemmte die Arme in die Seite und drehte sich langsam um. Schnell zog Edzard den Kopf hinter den Dosenstapel zurück. Kam der Mann auf ihn zu?

The road ended there. Railway tracks cut across Fiona's path. They carried on as a bridge for the trains across the water. Behind it was a second bridge for cars and pedestrians. Just then she heard a plink-plink sound, and saw the huge bridges move slowly upwards. They looked magnificent, like giant crocodiles opening their mouths for a yawn. Three boats chugged through the opening. After a while the majestic steel crocodiles gradually closed their jaws again.

Edzard wagte noch einen Blick. Der Mann kam tatsächlich auf ihn zu. Nichts wie weg hier! Er sprang auf, warf dabei einige der Öldosen um, schob den Vorhang beiseite, rutschte auf den Fliesen aus, als er um die Ecke bog, raste zum Fenster, stieß dabei gegen die Verpackungsmaschine, zog sich aus dem Fenster, sprang aufs Rad – gut, dass er es nicht abgeschlossen hatte –, trat in die Pedale, was das Zeug hielt, und jagte los, ohne sich umzudrehen.

It had started to rain. No point in going further, said Fiona to herself, I might as well cross over the bridge and go home. When she got to the other side of the water she looked back at the bridges once more. Lucky she had been there at the right time to see them opening. Suddenly something came charging into her, sending her and her bicycle flying. She landed with a bang. «Ouch!» She looked around. A fellow about her age had cycled straight into her. «Bloody hell!» Fiona shouted. «Can't you look where you're going? Stupid idiot.»

Edzard war mit Volldampf in Richtung Brücke gefahren. Gerade als er in die Uferstraße einbiegen wollte, war ihm ein Rad in die Quere gekommen. Er konnte nicht mehr bremsen oder ausweichen und war voll in das Rad hineingekachelt. Beide waren zu Boden gegangen. Mist! Bloody hell, rief dessen Fahrerin und dann noch etwas, was er nicht verstand. Die gehört zu dem Irren, der hinter ihm her war, durchfuhr es Edzard. Er blutete am linken Arm. Was jetzt? Er sprang auf, griff sein Fahrrad – es funktionierte noch – und fuhr davon.

Fiona just couldn't believe it. She had often heard that the Germans were rude, but this was too much. Not only did he crash into her after cycling like a madman, not only did he not apologize or ask her if she was all right or anything, but he even had the cheek to race off as if she was going to chase after him or something. She picked herself up and looked to see if there was any damage done. Only a bit of dust and a scratch or two. She'd survive, but the bike was pretty battered. She would have to push it home. That was it! She had had enough. She would talk to her father that night. Either he was going to spend more time with her and they'd have a proper holiday together, or else she would go back. Even boarding school during the summer holidays couldn't be worse than this place.

Edzard raste über die Brücke, fuhr rechts an der Telefonzelle vorbei in Richtung Stadt, dann gleich wieder rechts zum Holzlager. Es gab da ein verlassenes Stück, voller wilder Pflanzen, voll von Abfall und altem Eisen. Von dort aus konnte man das Gelände der *Friesland Fisch* überblicken.

Pushing her bike along the water Fiona looked back. She saw the fellow who had just crashed into her climbing through the wooden shutters she had passed by on the other side of the water. He was going into the yard with all the old rubble. She shook her head. Crazy, she thought, just crazy.

Detective Games

Fiona turned around. The fellow was pretending to look at the books on the table outside the shop. She walked away quickly, turning into another street and around the next corner. A few minutes later she saw that he was still following her. What the hell did this idiot want?

Since she had left the house that morning she had noticed that he was never very far away, and now it was pretty obvious that he was shadowing her. She marched straight up to him. «Was willst du?» she demanded.

Edzard wurde rot. «Wie meinst du das, was will ich? Ich habe doch gar nichts gesagt.»

Fiona was angry. «Gar nichts gesagt, aber … aber …» Shit! This bloody language. To hell with it, she'd just have to try it in English. «You've been following me all day long. I mean it's bad enough you having crashed into me on the bicycle yesterday and then having raced off without saying a word, but if you want to apologize, you don't really have to follow me around all day to do so.»

«Sorry», entschuldigte sich Edzard. Er zögerte einen Moment. «I didn't want to make you sick», fuhr er fort. Fiona had to smile. «Make me sick? What do you mean?»

«Verstehst du mich, wenn ich Deutsch rede?», fragte er zurück.

«Yeah, more or less.»

«Ich wollte sagen, dass ich dich nicht kränken wollte.»

«You didn't want to annoy me. O. k., but then why were you following me?»

Als Entschuldigung und Entschädigung für sein Benehmen am Vortag lud Edzard sie zu einem Eis ein. Bevor er ihre Frage beantwortete, wollte er erst selber ein paar stellen. «Bist wohl Engländerin, wie?»

«Do you think the English are the only ones who speak that language?» Fiona answered back. «No, I'm not English.»

«Amerikanerin?»

«Try again.»

Edzard dachte nach. Wo wurde denn sonst noch Englisch gesprochen? «Australierin? Südafrikanerin?»

«No, nothing as exotic as that!»

«Wo kommst du *denn* her?» Edzard fiel nichts mehr ein.

«Have you ever noticed the small island on the other side of Britain?» Fiona gave him a hint.

«Eine Irin, natürlich!»

«Well, you wouldn't have won a prize in a quiz, but now you know.»

Edzard überlegte, wie er am besten vorgehen sollte, ohne ihren Verdacht zu wecken. «Ich kann mir nicht vorstellen, dass es in Emden viele Iren gibt. Gibt es hier denn überhaupt andere Leute, die Englisch sprechen?», fragte er so beiläufig wie möglich.

«I haven't met any yet», answered Fiona, «except my father, of course!»

Viel zu schnell und direkt fragte Edzard: «Und wie sieht er aus?»

What kind of an idiot was this? She thought he was trying to make up for yesterday's accident, but instead of saying why he was following her, he was the one who was asking all kinds of funny questions. Like what her father looked like. «What does *your* father look like?» she asked back.

«Wieso?»

«Well, why do you want to know about mine?»

Jetzt muss mir schnell eine gute Ausrede einfallen, sonst stehe ich schon wieder dumm da, dachte Edzard. «Na ja, ich … äh, äh, ich finde, äh, ich finde nur, dass du überhaupt nicht wie eine typische Irin aussiehst, und will bloß wissen, wie das bei deinem Vater ist.» Klingt schwach, musste er sich selbst eingestehen.

«And what does a typically Irish person look like?» Fiona wanted to know. He's probably going to say something about red hair and freckles now, she thought.

«Hm. Ich würde sagen … rotes Haar und Sommersprossen!»

Fiona laughed. «I thought so», she said. «Well, as you can see, I'm blond and have no freckles. My father hasn't got any freckles either and he has light brown hair.»

«Ach, nicht schwarz?»

«What gave you that idea?»

«Nur so», antwortete Edzard erleichtert. Also war der Englisch sprechende Einbrecher vom vorherigen Abend nicht der Vater von diesem Mädchen. Ich glaub, ich möchte doch lieber kein Detektiv sein, dachte er, es ist ganz schön schwierig, Antworten auf Fragen zu bekommen, ohne die Fragen direkt zu stellen.

«I think it's my turn to ask a few questions now», Fiona decided to take the matter in hand. «First of all, what's your name?»

«Edzard», lautete die Antwort.

«Edward?» she asked.

«Nein, ED-ZARD.»

Fiona tried to say it a few times. «I've never heard that name before», she remarked.

«Ein alter ostfriesischer Name», erklärte Edzard stolz. «Unser größter Häuptling früher hieß so.»

«And I'm called Fiona. The red hair and freckles might be missing but the name is very Irish. Anyway, where were you racing to yesterday when you knocked me off my bike?»

Edzard holte tief Luft, dann erzählte er vom aufgeschnittenen Fliegendraht, vom offen stehenden Fenster, von dem Mann, der in den Fischfässern herumwühlte, und davon, dass er plötzlich ganz schnell wegrennen musste, weil er dachte, der Mann sei hinter ihm her. «Und als ich losgepest bin, na, da sind wir eben zusammengestoßen.»

«We didn't crash into each other», Fiona corrected, «*you* cycled straight into *me*. I was just cycling along minding my own business.»

«Na gut, kann sein, dass ich dich angefahren habe. Tut mir ja auch Leid. Und ich konnte dir nicht mal helfen, weil ich dachte, der Typ ist direkt hinter mir. Und außerdem ...» Er hielt mitten im Satz inne. «What *außerdem*?» Fiona queried.

«Hm, na ja, als du hingeknallt bist, da hast du irgendetwas auf Englisch geschimpft. Das hatte der Einbrecher auch, und ich dachte, dass ...»

«... that I had something to do with him. I see», she said thoughtfully, «what does he look like anyway?» Edzard musste nicht lange überlegen. «Er ist ziemlich groß, elegant gekleidet und hat schwarzes Haar», sagte er, stolz auf seine Beobachtungsgabe.

«Black hair», Fiona said slowly, «is that why you asked whether my father … you mean you thought … you thought … it was my Dad! That explains why you were following me around like a third-rate detective all day. I've never heard anything more ridiculous in all my life!» Fiona was really angry now. She stood up and turned to walk out of the door.

«Fiona, es tut mir Leid, bitte glaub mir», bat Edzard, «außerdem ist die Geschichte noch nicht zu Ende. Du verstehst sicher, warum ich mich heute so komisch benommen habe, wenn du den Rest hörst.»

Fiona sat down again. Was she mad listening to this fellow who obviously had a larger portion of fantasy than was good for him? On the other hand, she had nothing else to do, so why not?

«Also, als ich festgestellt hatte, dass der Typ nicht hinter mir hergelaufen war, bin ich zur Telefonzelle gegangen und habe den Chef von *Friesland Fisch* angerufen. Ich weiß, wie der heißt, weil meine Cousine früher da gearbeitet hat. Er ist schnell gekommen, und wir sind zusammen in die Fabrik gegangen. Das Fenster war inzwischen zu, aber man sah noch, dass der Fliegendraht aufgeschnitten war. Bloß in der großen Halle, da war alles wie verhext. Der Mann war weg, klar, aber es gab überhaupt keine Spuren, keine einzige, alles war wieder aufgeräumt. Und ich hatte Herrn Janssen vorher natürlich von den umgeworfenen Fässern und den Fischen auf dem Fußboden erzählt!»

«Yeah, you said that the place was in an awful mess when he was throwing the stuff around», Fiona remembered.

«Eben», fuhr Edzard fort, «und dann – nichts. Ich verstehe das auch nicht. Na ja. Herr Janssen war natürlich entsprechend sauer, nachdem er alles gecheckt und gesehen hatte, dass nichts fehlte. Er fragte nur, warum wohl jemand Fischfässer umkippen würde, bloß um hinterher alles wieder sauber aufzuräumen.»

«Well, you must admit that it sounds a bit unlikely», Fiona remarked.

«Unwahrscheinlich, ja, aber ich habe es doch gesehen! Glaubst du mir etwa nicht?»

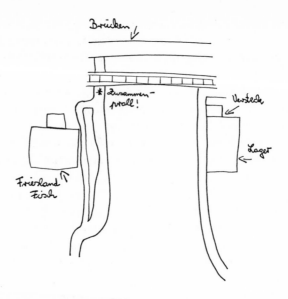

Fiona paused. «I don't know. Why should anyone root around in barrels full of fish?»

«Weiß ich doch nicht», sagte Edzard laut, «aber irgendeinen Sinn muss es doch haben.»

Fiona thought for a moment. «And you say the man was cursing in English?»

«Ja.»

«Where is this factory anyway?»

«Du musst doch vorbeigefahren sein nach unserem, äh, Zusammentreffen.» Er nahm eine Serviette und begann, mit seinem Filzschreiber eine Skizze zu zeichnen. «Hier sind die Brücken. Hier die Eisenbahnbrücke und dahinter die für Autos und Fußgänger. Über die bist du gefahren. Untendrunter natürlich das Wasser. Hier auf dem rechten Ufer sind die Lager, und hier ist der Platz, wo ich mich versteckt hab. Lauter Müll und ...»

«Yes, I saw the place yesterday when I cycled there», Fiona interrupted him impatiently, «and where is the mysterious fish factory?»

«Also, auf der anderen Seite geht dieser Weg am Ufer lang.

Bei diesem Kreuz sind wir zusammengeknallt, äh, Entschuldigung, habe ich dich angefahren. Ich bin aus dieser Straße rausgerast. Das Gebäude hier ist die *Friesland Fisch*-Fabrik. Soll ich sie dir nicht lieber *live* zeigen?»

«If you like», Fiona replied. She didn't know whether or not she was really interested, but she had nothing else planned. «Will we go there now?» she asked.

«Lieber nicht», meinte Edzard, «Herr Janssen wird jetzt in seinem Büro sein, und ich möchte ihm nicht unbedingt über den Weg laufen. Mann, war der gestern sauer! Ich hatte ihn aus seiner Doppelkopfrunde rausgeholt. Am besten warten wir bis heute Abend.»

«What was he doing with two heads yesterday? This story is getting stranger and stranger.» Fiona was puzzled.

«Nicht mit zwei Köpfen!», lachte Edzard. «Doppelkopf ist ein Kartenspiel. Echt spannend.»

«O. k., so where will we meet tonight?» Fiona wanted to know.

Edzard überlegte. «Wenn wir uns vor dem Kino treffen, fällt es nicht so auf. Sagen wir mal so um halb acht?»

«Which cinema?»

«Es gibt nur eins. Weißt du, wo das ist?»

«Well, if there's only one then I know it», said Fiona. This fellow really was a bit crazy, she thought. Who was going to notice if they met anywhere? Oh well, she'd see this evening what the fish plant was like and if the wire really had been cut open or not. If not, she'd know he had made it all up.

On her way home she passed the cinema. An over-18-film was showing there called *Heiße Mädchen, wildes Fleisch*. Oh God, she thought for a moment, hopefully the whole thing isn't some stupid excuse to get me to go to the pictures with him …

Fisch, nicht Fleisch

«Look Fiona, I said I was sorry, but there's nothing I can do. I'm sure there's a nice film on telly that you can watch. See you later, pet.»

Fiona put the phone down. She knew it was her father when she had heard it ringing. Working late again, even though he had promised her only the day before that he would try to spend more time with her. Things were hectic at work at the moment, he had said.

She'd eat her tea alone in front of the television that evening. German television. She'd love to see something in English. Or even better, to have tea with her father again. Oh well, maybe it wasn't too bad that he wasn't home today. That way she wouldn't have to say anything about where she was going and who she was meeting.

Edzard war schon um zwanzig nach sieben am Kino. Als er sah, was gespielt wurde, wartete er lieber etwas weiter entfernt. Es sollte nicht so aussehen, als ob er ins «Wilde Fleisch» gehen wollte. Punkt halb acht kam Fiona.

«Toll, dass du jetzt schon da bist», sagte Edzard, «erst hinterher ist mir eingefallen, dass du vielleicht eine Stunde später kommen würdest – ihr habt doch so komische Zeiten in England. *Half eight* ist bei euch doch acht Uhr dreißig, oder?»

«First of all I don't come from England, and anyway, it's you lot who have got the time all wrong. But our German teacher warned us about it, so I knew that you really meant half seven when you said *halb acht*», she said with a grin. They cycled off towards the Delft.

Ein paar Minuten später konnte Edzard erklären: «So, hier links: die geheimnisvolle *Friesland Fisch*. Hinter der großen Einfahrt ist die Halle mit den Maschinen und dem Lager, und da drüben sind die Büros. Und hier ... komisch ... das Gitter ist schon wieder ...»

He didn't finish the sentence. Just then they heard a noise

coming from inside the building. Edzard wurde bleich. «Was machen wir jetzt?»

Fiona was looking around. «Hide somewhere. Quick, come on!» Sie rannten mit den Fahrrädern zu einem großen Stapel Paletten.

They hadn't even caught their breath when a man appeared at the window. He looked around before climbing out carefully. Then he got into a car parked nearby and drove away. «Los, schnell, hinter ihm her», rief Edzard und radelte los.

«You're mad, he's too fast in a car», Fiona shouted, but Edzard was already gone. She jumped onto her bike and rode after him.

«Scheiße», japste Edzard, als er schließlich anhielt, weil er das Auto aus den Augen verloren hatte, «nun ist er weg. Hast du dir die Autonummer merken können?»

Fiona was puffed too. She wiped the sweat from her forehead. «Well, the letters were AUR, I think, then B. And the numbers...»

«AUR, das heißt, das Auto ist in Aurich angemeldet», warf Edzard ein.

«... three, seven, five. Those were the numbers», Fiona concluded. – «Nicht drei, fünf, sieben?», fragte Edzard. «Meiner Meinung nach war das drei, fünf, sieben.»

Fiona frowned. «I don't think so, but I'm not sure.»

«Also, ein grüner Golf mit dem Kennzeichen AUR-B-357 oder 375. Ich glaube nicht, dass uns das weit bringen wird.»

They started walking. Edzard was pushing his bicycle on the road, Fiona was beside him with her bike on the footpath. She stopped dead in her tracks.

«What do you mean that won't bring us very far? Who's *us*? Do you think I want to get involved in this? Anyway, it's not really any of our business, is it?»

She walked on. Edzard sah sie von der Seite an. Vielleicht hatte sie Recht. Eigentlich ging es sie ja wirklich nichts an. Aber da musste doch etwas dahinter stecken. Er hätte zu gerne gewusst, was. «Na ja, ich dachte nur ... ich dachte, es interessiert dich auch.» Er klang enttäuscht. «Aber klar, wenn du nichts damit zu tun haben willst ...»

Fiona had a suggestion to make. «Why don't you phone this Herr Janssen fellow and tell him what you saw? That's probably the best thing to do.»

«Ja, sicher», antwortete Edzard ironisch, «erstens wird er mir nicht glauben, dass schon wieder jemand da war. Und wenn, dann würden wir sicher wieder keine Spuren finden. Nein, danke. Einmal reicht. Außerdem, warum um alles auf der Welt sollte nun noch einer einbrechen?»

Fiona stopped again. «Wait a minute. You mean that man just now wasn't the one you saw yesterday?» She was getting interested in spite of herself.

«Natürlich nicht! Der von gestern hatte doch schwarzes Haar und wirkte insgesamt sehr elegant. Und den gerade hast du doch selber gesehen: blond mit alten Jeans und Parka. Ein ganz anderer Typ, sag ich dir.»

Fiona was amazed. «What are they all looking for in there?» she asked. Edzard grinste. «Möchte ich auch gerne wissen!»

Sie liefen noch eine Weile durch die Straßen, sahen die Menschen in die Kneipen gehen und Paare sich treffen. Die Punks hingen an ihrem Lieblingsplatz gegenüber dem Rathaus herum.

«I think I'll head off home now», said Fiona after a while, «my father should be finished work and hell be wondering where I am.» It was o. k. walking around with Edzard, but she didn't really know what they should do now.

«Alles klar», erwiderte Edzard. Blöder Spruch eigentlich, dachte er, schön nichts sagend. Aber was soll man denn sonst antworten? Auf einmal legte er seine Hand auf Fionas Arm und hielt sie zurück. Seine Augen wurden ganz groß. «Mensch!», flüsterte er. «Mensch, da ist er. Guck dir mal den Mann da an. Das ist der von gestern!» Ein gepflegter, schwarzhaariger Herr betrat gerade eine Kneipe.

A few minutes later Fiona walked into the same pub. She pretended she was looking for someone and took her time inspecting the place. Most of the tables were full. Groups of friends chatting noisily, people smoking, couples sitting very close together talking intimately. She couldn't see the black-haired fellow anywhere. She was just about to leave the pub when she noticed the stairs, which led down to the toilets. At the top of them, in a little niche, was the telephone. The man was standing there, receiver in hand, talking to someone. She went towards the stairs as if she was going to go down to the ladies.

«I'm telling you», she heard him saying, «there was nothing in them. Something's gone wrong. I'll have to hang around here for a while. A fucking pain it is. Maybe Freddy got there before us ... You're going to come over here yourself? ... Yeah, maybe that's best ... See you then. Bye.»

He was an Irishman! Fiona was shocked. She thought he would be American or English, not Irish. But it was clear from his accent. Somewhere from the south of Ireland – Cork maybe, or Kerry.

Was macht die bloß da drin? So lange kann das doch nicht dauern. Edzard trat von einem Bein aufs andere. Der Kerl kann eigentlich nicht ahnen, dass sie weiß, wer er ist, oder? Edzard wurde nervös. Endlich kam Fiona wieder heraus. Sie erzählte, was sie gehört hatte und dass der Mann Ire war. Kaum war sie fertig, da verließ der Schwarzhaarige die Kneipe und ging direkt auf sie zu. «Er kann doch nicht wissen ...», flüsterte Edzard.

«Will we run?» Fiona asked.

«Lieber nicht. Warten wir's ab», entschied Edzard.

Der Mann kam tatsächlich direkt auf sie zu. «Hello», he said, «do you speak English?» Fiona shook her head to say no. He shouldn't hear that she was Irish, too. «Nein», she said quietly. «A little bit», sagte Edzard. «Good», continued the man, «I was wondering if you could help me.»

Er schien Edzard nicht zu erkennen. Oder war das ein Trick? Hatte er ihn doch gesehen, als er am Abend zuvor weggerannt war?

«I need some change for the cigarette machine and I only have a ten mark note.» Edzard holte sein Kleingeld heraus und wechselte. «Here you are», sagte er. «Thanks very much», replied the man. He looked at the two of them and grinned. «Have a nice evening.» Fiona blushed.

Strange News

Bäng. Bäng. Bäng. Drei Hammerschläge. Der Richter erhob sich. «Hiermit verurteile ich Big Freddy zu zehn Jahren Haft wegen Fischspionage. An dieser Stelle möchte ich besonders den Mut und die Tapferkeit von Edzard Mayners hervorheben. Ohne ihn wäre es nie zu diesem Prozess gekommen.» Edzard wurde verlegen und wehrte das Lob mit einer Handbewegung ab. Aber er war natürlich stolz.

Bäng. Bäng. Bäng. Wieso klopfte der Richter noch einmal? «Edzard!», rief eine Stimme. «Edzard, steh doch auf!» Langsam wachte Edzard auf. O nein! Die alte Zicke war wieder da. Die Super-Überwacherin. Schlimmer als jeder Polizist.

Er stand auf, zog schnell seinen Bademantel an und ging zur Tür. «Moin, Frau Heerma», brummte er. «Moin, Edzard. Es ist schon halb zehn. Höchste Zeit, dass du aufstehst. Hier ist die Zeitung. Ich war schon einkaufen und habe sie von unten hochgebracht. Und frische Brötchen und Milch habe ich auch für dich. Du isst wahrscheinlich nichts anderes als deine Matjes, wenn du alleine gelassen wirst. Ich will nicht, dass es später heißt, ich hätte nicht auf dich Acht gegeben.» Das passiert be-

«Morning, pet.» Fionas father gave her a kiss. He had set the table for breakfast. «Sleep well?» – «Yeah», muttered Fiona and added, «I didn't hear you coming in last night. You must have been very late.» He really spent his life at work, she thought.

«It was after midnight but we got it sorted out in the end. Once something goes wrong with the computer, it takes ages to find out what it is. I'm taking the morning off today, so we can have a nice late breakfast together.»

He asked her what she had done the evening before. She said that she had cycled around a bit and had then come home and looked at television.

«Anything good on?» her father wanted to

stimmt nicht, dachte Edzard düster. Er war noch ziemlich verschlafen.

Während sie sprach, versuchte sie die ganze Zeit, an Edzard vorbei in die Wohnung zu spähen. Die will wohl wissen, ob sie total ramponiert ist. Als Nächstes wird sie bestimmt fragen, ob sie mir nicht beim Saubermachen helfen kann, dachte er. Dieser Gedanke besserte seine Laune nicht gerade.

«Wenn du willst, dass ich dir beim Saubermachen helfe, sag ruhig Bescheid», bot ihm Frau Heerma prompt an.

«Danke, aber ich komme schon zurecht. Sie brauchen wirklich nichts für mich tun», antwortete Edzard. Frau Heerma schüttelte den Kopf: «Ich muss sagen, ich finde das immer noch nicht richtig, so einen jungen Kerl ganz allein in der Wohnung zu lassen. Wenn ich deine Mutter wäre ...»

Bist du aber nicht, Gott sei Dank, sagte er sich in Gedanken und laut zu der neugierigen Nachbarin: «Wir haben schon oft darüber geredet, Frau Heerma, ich glaube nicht, dass es einen Sinn hat. Vielen Dank für die Brötchen und die Milch.» So höflich wie möglich machte Edzard die Tür zu.

Zum ersten Mal waren seine Eltern ohne ihn in Urlaub gefahren, und er durfte allein zu Hause bleiben. Aber

know. «No, boring as usual.» Mr. Burke worried about his daughter. She didn't know anyone in Emden and had to spend quite a lot of time alone. «One of my colleagues at work, Herr Backhuysen, has a daughter about your age called Hilke», he said, «she is having a few friends around tomorrow afternoon. He said you could go along if you wanted to.» He looked for the address in his pocket. «At about four o'clock, I think he said.» He found the pieces of paper and gave it to her.

Once a week *The Irish Times* arrived in the post. The Saturday's edition. Fiona read the latest news from home while her father looked through the *Ostfriesen-Zeitung.*

Suddenly he laughed. «That's odd», he said, «can you imagine

diese Hilfspolizistin wollte ihm alles verderben. Es könnte so viel Spaß machen, wenn bloß nicht ständig diese Kontrollen wären: ob er genug zu essen hat; ob er richtig sauber macht; ob sie nicht seine Wäsche mitwaschen soll? Warum konnte sie ihn nicht in Ruhe lassen! Edzard seufzte und vertiefte sich erst mal in die Zeitung.

someone breaking into a fish processing plant just to throw the fish around?» Fiona stared at him. «Fish?» she asked, trying to sound as innocent as possible. «Let me see.»

Wer klaut schon tote Fische?

Eine böse Überraschung erlebte Johann Janssen, der Besitzer der *Friesland Fisch,* als er gestern Abend noch in seiner Firma nach dem Rechten sah. Vandalen schienen dort gehaust zu haben. Auf dem Boden, überall verstreut, Fische, leere Fässer, Salzlauge. Ein Teil einer Ladung Heringe aus Irland war ausgekippt worden. «Das muss ein Verrückter gewesen sein», erklärte der verstörte Herr Janssen unserem Reporter, «denn wer klaut schon Fische?» Bis Redaktionsschluss konnte noch nicht festgestellt werden, ob etwas fehlte. Einen Sabotageakt der Konkurrenz – die *Friesland Fisch* hatte in letzter Zeit mit abgepackten echten Matjesfilets in verschiedenen Saucen für Aufsehen gesorgt und mehrere Preise erhalten – schließt Herr Janssen aus.

Edzard war erstaunt. Der Blonde musste also auch etwas in den Fässern gesucht haben. Aber was, zum Teufel? Doch keine toten Fische. Offensichtlich war er nicht so or-

Fiona couldn't help it. Somehow she was fascinated by the whole thing. An Irishman in Emden

dentlich wie der Schwarzhaarige. Ob Fiona den Bericht auch gelesen hatte? Blöde Frage. Warum sollte sie ausgerechnet die *Ostfriesen-Zeitung* lesen? Und außerdem, die Sache hatte sie so kalt gelassen, dass sie sich nicht mal für einen der nächsten Tage verabredet hatten. Für sie war er wahrscheinlich gestorben. Schade. Jemand, der perfekt Englisch sprach, wäre in diesem Fall eine große Hilfe gewesen. Fall, was für ein Fall, bremste Edzard sich, während er sich ein Matjesfilet aufs Brötchen legte und zubiss.

looking for fish or something hidden in fish barrels which had come over from Ireland, and someone else – probably a German or at least someone with a car from the area – looking for the same thing. She had made no arrangement with Edzard to meet again soon, she didn't even know his phone number or anything, but she felt like talking to him again. Especially now that it was in the papers. Where could she meet him? She remembered the place where they had had an ice-cream together. It was worth a try.

«Fiona! So ein Zufall. Ich wollte gerade ein Eis essen.» Edzard tat überrascht.

«Yes, it's quite a coincidence all right», lied Fiona, who had just finished her second milk-shake wondering if he would come along. But she didn't want him to know that she had been waiting. «Why don't you join me? I was just about to order an ice-cream, too. Did you see the report in the *Ostfriesen-Zeitung* today?»

Edzard setzte sich. «Was denn? Du liest 'ne deutsche Zeitung! Hätte ich ja nie gedacht.»

«Well», Fiona admitted, «my father does. And he showed me the article about the break-in at *Friesland Fisch*.»

Edzard fragte, ob sie ihrem Vater vom vorherigen Abend erzählt hatte, und fand es nicht erstaunlich, dass sie nichts gesagt hatte. «Ich würde meinen Alten auch nichts davon erzählen. Zum Glück sind sie ja jetzt weg und machen Ferien, da kann ich kommen und gehen, wie ich will.» Das hört sich doch toll an, dachte er und erwartete zumindest einen neidischen Blick von Fiona. Die reagierte aber gar nicht.

«Has that Herr Janssen been in touch with you?» she changed the subject.

«Warum das denn?», gab Edzard erstaunt zurück.

«Well, if you tell him one evening that his place has been broken into and that there's fish lying all over the place and he goes there and sees nothing, and then suddenly, the next night, he finds exactly what you described the night before, he must think it's a bit fishy.» Fiona grinned. «Oops, sorry, I mean a bit funny!»

Edzard wurde nachdenklich: «Da haste eigentlich recht. Hoffentlich denkt er nicht, ich hätte was damit zu tun.»

«And do you know what the awful thing about it is?» Fiona continued. Edzard schüttelte den Kopf. «If he asks you where you were at the time of the break-in. You do remember where you were, don't you?»

Edzard wurde flau im Magen. «O Gott. Ja. Aber du warst ja auch da. Du bist meine Zeugin. Und wir haben den gesehen, der es getan hat.»

«Yeah, sure», said Fiona sarcastically, «do you think he'll believe you? First of all you tell him a fairy tale the night before when nothing happened, and now you want him to believe that you were at the factory – by pure coincidence – when it was broken into the second time. He'll ask why you didn't phone him.»

Edzard sah sehr unglücklich aus. «Verdammter Mist! Was

machen wir jetzt, ich meine, was mach ich jetzt?», verbesserte er sich. Schließlich wollte Fiona nichts mit dem Fall zu tun haben. Oder hatte sie ihre Meinung geändert?

«I suggest we finish our ice-creams and go for a long walk by the water to talk about it. You never know who might overhear you in this place», she said like a professional detective. Or so she thought. Until she looked around and saw there was no one else in the ice-cream parlour.

Zehn Minuten später befanden sie sich auf dem Weg zum Delft. Es war ein schöner Tag. Sonnenschein und Wind. Genau wie Edzard es gerne mochte. «Ich habe dich noch gar nicht gefragt, wieso du in Emden bist. Arbeitet dein Vater hier, oder was?»

Fiona sighed. «Yes. And he works too bloody much. I hardly ever see him. I suppose that's what Germany does to you. Anyway, I came over ...» Fiona didn't finish her sentence. They were passing by a newspaper kiosk where a woman was standing shouting: «Matches, matches!»

«O Mann, ich dreh gleich durch!», stöhnte Edzard. «Wieso will die denn an einem Zeitungskiosk Matjes kaufen? Wieso ist die ganze Welt auf einmal wild nach Fisch?»

«She doesn't want to buy fish, you idiot, look at what she's doing», replied Fiona.

Die Frau steckte sich eine Zigarette zwischen die Lippen und deutete damit an, dass sie Feuer brauchte. «Natürlich, Streichhölzer will sie haben!», lachte Edzard. Zur gleichen Zeit kapierte das auch der Zeitungsverkäufer.

Fiona took Edzard by the hand and pulled him around the next corner. «Was hast du?», wollte er wissen. Fiona sah ziemlich verwirrt aus. «Do you know where that woman is from?» she asked him. «Ireland! What the hell are all these Irish people doing in Emden all of a sudden?»

The Project

Für den Nachmittag hatten sie sich im Versteck verabredet. When Fiona arrived, Edzard was there already, equipped with a pair of binoculars. «Wow, look at the super detective's kit!» she slagged him. Edzard sagte nichts. «What are you going to do now?» Fiona asked.

«Von hier aus kann man alles überblicken. Ich warte, bis die wiederkommen», erklärte Edzard ihr seinen Plan.

«Hm.» Fiona wasn't convinced. «Would *you* come back here again after you'd read about the break-in in the paper? I think we're wasting our time if we hang around waiting for something like that to happen.»

«Du weißt ja noch nicht das Neueste», belehrte sie Edzard, «als ich heute Mittag nach Hause gefahren bin ...»

«... you saw a creature from outer space breaking into the fish plant!»

Edzard fand das nicht witzig. «Halt doch mal die Klappe und hör zu!» Fiona wondered what she was supposed to hold while she was listening to him. «Also, als ich nach Hause gefahren bin, ich glaub, da hab ich gesehen, wie der Schwarzhaarige den blonden Typ mit dem Auto gesehen und sich sofort versteckt hat.»

«What? The fellow who made the phone call, the first burglar, saw the one who broke in after him? And he didn't want to be seen by him?»

«Ja.»

«Are you sure?», Fiona wanted to know.

«Nicht ganz. Das war auf der Hauptstraße. Ich war schon vorbeigefahren, und es hatte sozusagen rückwärts in meinem Kopf geklingelt. Und als ich mich umdrehte, waren sie schon nicht mehr zu sehen.»

«And did you cycle back?»

«Ja. Leider ohne Erfolg. Aber wenn beide noch in der Stadt sind, dann haben sie vielleicht noch nichts gefunden, was immer das ist, hinter dem sie her sind. Und deshalb warte ich hier», erklärte Edzard. «Außerdem wissen wir doch, dass der schwarzhaarige Typ vom Sonntag, der wieder aufgeräumt hat, kein Deutsch kann. Der hat den Artikel bestimmt nicht gelesen.»

«And the second one, the one with the Aurich car?» Fiona asked.

«Ob das Freddy ist?»

«Why?»

«Na ja, der Schwarzhaarige hat doch am Telefon gesagt: ‹Maybe Freddy got there before us.› Und wenn da nicht noch mehr Leute einen Wettbewerb im Fischfässerumkippen machen, dann müsste Freddy doch der Typ mit dem Auto sein.»

Fiona shook her head. «That was too quick and too long for me», she sighed. «You think the second fellow is called Freddy, is that right?»

Edzard nickte. «Also wir wissen bisher: Irgendwas muss in den Fässern sein. Der Schwarzhaarige und Freddy wollen es beide haben. Aber es ist wohl noch nicht da. Deshalb schlage ich vor, dass wir einfach abwarten und *Friesland Fisch* von hier aus beobachten.»

«I still don't think they'll come back», Fiona insisted.

«Und was schlägst du vor, Mrs. Schlauberger?», knurrte Edzard.

«Miss Schlauberger, if you please. I think I'll go in there and have a look around.» Fiona stared at him cheekily.

«Was heißt, you go in there?»

«You'll go in there», she corrected.

Edzard machte eine abwehrende Handbewegung. «Ich hab Ferien. Lenk nicht ab. Wie willst du denn da reinkommen?»

«Well, I could …» she hesitated. «I'm from an Irish newspaper!»

«Ha, ha», lachte Edzard höhnisch, «darf ich bitte Ihren Presseausweis sehen, junge Frau?»

«Well, then I'm … Shit! … I'm … I've got it!» she declared. «I'm doing a project for school. I'll just say that everyone in my class has to do a project about something, which is in some way connected with Ireland and the place where we spent our holidays. And I want to find out what happens to an Irish herring before it ends up on a German dinner table. To find that out, I have to interview the boss!» She was pleased with her idea.

«Wirst du nie schaffen.» Edzard war sich seiner Sache sicher.

«Bet you», Fiona snapped back and walked off.

«Wo gehst du denn hin?», rief er ihr nach.

«To the nearest phone-box», she shouted back over her shoulder.

Zwanzig Minuten später traute Edzard seinen Augen kaum. Durch sein Fernglas sah er Fiona auf dem Weg zu *Friesland Fisch,* einen großen Notizblock unter dem Arm. Ganz schön selbstbewusst, dachte er anerkennend, hoffentlich muss ich sie da nicht raushauen.

Herr Janssen, a friendly, dynamic man in his early thirties, had just put down the phone when Fiona came into his office.

«Moin», he greeted her, «you're the girl from Ireland, aren't you? We do a lot of business with Ireland.»

«Es ist sehr nett, dass Sie haben sofort Zeit für mich», answered Fiona, «und Sie können ruhig Deutsch zu mir sprechen.»

«Gut», said Herr Janssen. «Ich rede Deutsch and you can speak English if you want to, o. k.?»

«O. k.», Fiona nodded. There was a pause. She didn't really know how to start. «I read in the paper that someone broke in here and stole some fish», she began.

«Ach, das interessiert dich?» Did he stare at her suspiciously as he said that? «Und ich dachte, es geht um die Reise des Herings von Irland hierher.»

«Yes, of course», Fiona added quickly, «it's just that I read about it in your local paper.»

«Es wurde übrigens nichts gestohlen; irgendein Irrer hat bloß die Fässer umgekippt. Ein Irrer, kein Ire!» He laughed. Fiona started to feel a bit uneasy.

«Ich glaub, das war so ein Bengel in deinem Alter», Herr

Janssen continued, «ruft am Abend vorher hier an und sagt, jemand hat die Heringsfässer umgekippt. Ich komm her, und nix ist. Wollte mich wohl auf den Arm nehmen, *pull my leg*, wie ihr in Irland sagt. Ich hab ihn natürlich zur Sau gemacht, äh, *I gave out to him.* Na ja, und am nächsten Tag waren dann tatsächlich die Fässer umgekippt, und da hat er nicht angerufen. Hat er sich wohl doch nicht getraut. Na, wenn ich den erwische! Den steck ich kopfüber in ein Fass mit Salzwasser.»

Fiona felt sick. Did he know everything? Wasn't he looking at her very critically?

«Egal», Herr Janssen went on, «komm, ich zeig dir mal, was wir hier machen.»

They went into a big hall. It must have been the one where it had all happened, Fiona thought, because she recognized the orange fork-lift trucks and the blue and green barrels from Edzard's description.

«Also, die frischen Heringe werden in Irland in diese Fässer geschüttet. Gleichzeitig kommt Salz obendrauf. Die Fässer bleiben dann meistens für einige Tage auf dem Kai stehen, je nach Witterung kürzer oder länger, und reifen dadurch, bevor sie abgeschickt werden.»

«Unprotected?» Fiona asked. «Then anyone could steal them.»

«Ihr habt wohl heutzutage alle zu viel Fernsehen gesehen», Herr Janssen shook his head, «kannst du mir mal einen vernünftigen Grund dafür sagen, dass jemand Fässer mit Fischen in Salzlake klaut?»

Fiona couldn't. But she would have liked to have known one. «And those herrings are made into matjes here, then?»

«Nein, aus denen werden Salzheringe. Heringe für Matjes kommen hier tiefgefroren an. Zurück zu den Fässern. Die werden dann in einen Container gepackt. Sie gehen per Schiff nach Rotterdam oder Bremerhaven und danach per LKW hierher. Bei uns werden sie entladen und auf Paletten gestellt, so wie hier.» He pointed to the stack of blue and green barrels.

«Why are some green and some blue?» she asked.

«Das bedeutet nichts», antwortete Herr Janssen, «hier, solche Stempel, die bedeuten was, K bezeichnet das Fanggebiet, 8/9 bezeichnet die Größe. So 'n Fass wiegt ungefähr 150 Kilo.»

150 kg, Fiona wrote down in her notebook. She was collecting material for her project, she had to remind herself. Herr Janssen nodded and continued:

«So, also zuerst kommen die Fische in diesen Apparat und werden gesäubert und entgrätet. Über ein Förderband geht's in den nächsten Raum. Dort werden sie unterschiedlich weiterverarbeitet. Wenn sie später als Salzheringe verkauft werden sollen», er zeigte auf eine Maschine, «laufen sie schnell hier durch und werden dann in Eimer verpackt.» Sie gingen weiter. «Und hier legen wir die Fische auf ein Sieb, sie tropfen ab, und wenn sie abgetropft sind, kommen sie auf ein Förderband und laufen in eine Maschine, die den Heringslappen die Haut abzieht; die Filets ohne Haut werden dann dahinten verpackt und …»

Fiona felt she couldn't take in any more information. But she hadn't really found out anything yet that would help Edzard and herself.

«What happens if something else is in the barrels – other than fish, I mean?» she asked.

Herr Janssen frowned. «Komische Frage, was soll denn in den Fässern anderes drin sein als Fisch?»

«A stone, maybe, or a shell», Fiona suggested.

«Na ja, an der Schneidemaschine gäb's Ärger, ein Stein würde eventuell ein Messer kaputtmachen. Auf jeden Fall hätten wir einen Riesenkrach. Aber der Stein würde wahrscheinlich vorher rausgewaschen. Und, wie gesagt, so was passiert nicht. Weißt du jetzt genug?»

«Oh yes, thank you. You have been very helpful», said Fiona. She closed her notebook where she had been taking down the information for her ‹project›.

«Gut, komm nochmal mit ins Büro, dann zeig ich dir auf der Karte die Transportwege.»

When they were in the office, the phone rang. «Oh, hello»,

Fiona heard Herr Janssen say, «no, they haven't arrived yet. Yes, they should have by now.» Fiona was all ears. She tried to listen carefully without looking as if she was.

«That's great that you're coming over yourself on Friday», he was saying, «we can talk it all over then. Bye.» Herr Janssen put down the phone and smiled at Fiona. «You see, this is a real bilingual business. That was an Irish *Geschäftsfreund*, äh, business friend.»

«A business associate or colleague, you mean», Fiona helped him. «I see. Well, thank you very much again. You've been very friendly and helpful. Most of my homework is done now.»

Im Versteck empfing Edzard sie mit Ungeduld. «Mensch, du warst ja ewig weg. Ich hatte schon überlegt, ob ich eingreifen soll.»

Fiona shook her head. «You and your fantasies. I know everything about fish processing now.»

«Und nichts Verdächtiges?»

«Not really, but here's some evidence for you», she said and handed him a plastic bag. «Herr Janssen gave it to me.»

Edzard packte aus. «Mensch, Wahnsinn! Matjes in feinstem Madeira, Matjes in Sahnesoße mit Äpfeln, Matjes, Matjes. Klasse! Oh, das wird 'ne Fressorgie!»

«You can be very easily bribed for a detective, can't you?» Fiona teased.

«Ja, richtig.» Er legte die Packungen zurück in die Plastiktüte. «Und sonst? Nun erzähl doch mal.»

Fiona gave a summary of what she had been told.

«Na bitte», unterbrach Edzard sie, als sie das Telefongespräch erwähnte, «da haben wir's. Das Zeug ist noch nicht hier, und der Boss aus Irland kommt selbst. Vielleicht ist der dieser Freddy.»

«Will you stop being so stupid, Edzard», Fiona said seriously. «Herr Janssen deals with fish. All it probably means is that a delivery didn't arrive on time and now his business associate is coming over here to see what happened. That's perfectly normal, you know. If he's involved in the whole thing, why would people break into his place? And anyway, what kind of *Zeug* are you thinking of?»

Edzard zuckte mit den Achseln. «Weiß ich doch auch nicht. Ich weiß nur, dass irgendwas nicht stimmt. Sonst nichts Auffälliges?»

«Nothing. That is, nothing except that around the corner from the fish place I saw a green Golf parked, with no one in it.» She opened her notebook. «The registration number is AUR-B-815.»

Hallo, Dolly!

Fiona turned right into Ubbo-Emmius-Straße. Number 23 was the house the Backhuysens lived in, her father had said. She really enjoyed cycling in Emden. The red bricks on the roads and the houses gave the town a warm, friendly atmosphere. The houses were nice, too. They didn't look all the same like they did on housing estates at home. She stopped in front of number 23. It was a lovely big house with a huge window full of plants in the front. She wondered what Hilke would be like.

Nobody came when she rang the bell. Was she at the wrong house? She rang again. Maybe Herr Backhuysen had forgotten to tell Hilke that she was coming. But he had told her father that a few friends were calling around ...

Fiona was just about to leave when a girl appeared. Her face was a bit red and her hair was ruffled. She was still closing the buttons of her blouse when she opened the door.

«Ja, bitte?» she asked.

«Guten Tag. Ich bin die Fiona.» The girl just stared at her. «Fiona Burke. Mein Vater und dein Vater arbeiten zusammen.» The girl raised on eyebrow.

«Ach ja, die Irin. Stimmt. Ich bin Hilke. Mein Alter sagte, du wolltest vorbeikommen.»

I didn't bloody well want to come – he asked me to, Fiona wanted to say, but before she could think of it in German, Hilke had turned back into the house. «Komm doch rein», she said over her shoulder.

In Hilke's room a good-looking fellow was lying on the bed. He looked Fiona up and down cooly and muttered: «Moin.»

«Fabian, das ist Fiona. Sie kommt aus Irland», sagte Hilke und setzte sich neben ihn aufs Bett.

It was an awful afternoon. The two of them just kept asking her questions all the time and didn't really listen to the answers. Fabian's hands kept trying to find a way inside Hilke's blouse, and she couldn't stop giggling and playing with his hair.

«Hast du denn keinen Freund?», «Was machst du hier die ganze Zeit?», fragten sie und: «Habe ich dich nicht gestern mit Matjes gesehen?»

«With who?» Fiona asked back.

«Na, mit Matjes Mayners. Wie heißt der nochmal richtig? Ach ja, Edzard!»

«Why do they call you ‹Matjes›?» Fiona asked Edzard later that afternoon when they met in their ice-cream parlour.

«Weil ich die so gerne esse», antwortete er.

«Ugg!» Fiona was disgusted. «How could you! Raw fish!»

«Erst probieren, dann meckern. Iss mal ein paar davon, dann redest du ganz anders.»

«No way!» she was sure. «It's bad enough chasing people who put their hands into barrels full of them. Anyway, how come you know Hilke or she knows you?»

«Hilke Backhuysen?», fragte Edzard. «Die ist in meiner Klasse, aber ich mag sie nicht besonders.» Nachdem Fiona ihm von ihrem Nachmittag bei ihr erzählt hatte, fügte er noch hinzu: «Und den Fabian, den Lackaffen, den kannst du auch vergessen.»

Nobody said anything for a moment. Dann fragte Edzard zum x-ten Mal: «Wie finden wir bloß raus, hinter was die Einbrecher her sind?»

«We could ask them», said Fiona ironically, «excuse me, please, aren't you one of the men who's looking for something in the barrels of fish? Would you be so kind as to tell us what it is?»

«Haha, irre komisch. Hast du noch so 'nen tollen Vorschlag?»

«Well, we could ask a spirit», she suggested.

«Einen was?» Spirit hieß Alkohol, so viel wusste er, aber sie wollte ja wohl kaum eine Flasche Whiskey ausfragen.

«A spirit», Fiona repeated, «a ghost, you know, someone who's dead.»

Jetzt verstand Edzard, was das Wort bedeutete, aber es ergab für ihn keinen Sinn. «Willst du dir einen im Friedhof aussuchen und ausgraben, oder wie?»

Fiona laughed. «No, nothing as messy as that. We don't need the old remains, it's the spirit which we want to help us. We could do it with a glass.»

Nicht der Geist aus der Flasche, sondern der Geist aus dem Glas. O Gott, mit wem hatte er sich da eingelassen? Total verblüfft fragte Edzard: «Hast du so was denn schon mal gemacht?»

«Of course», boasted Fiona, «one of the girls in my class in school is really into that sort of thing. Her mother is supposed to be a medium, and Helen says she's one, too. For a séance you need a medium, but not when you have a go at a ouija board. Helen has a ouija board hidden in her cupboard in school.»

Edzard verstand immer noch nur Bahnhof, wollte aber nicht schon wieder fragen. Fiona decided to tell him about it anyway.

«The ouija board has all the letters of the alphabet printed around the sides, and a place for *yes* and a place for *no*. Everyone who's there puts the index finger of their right hand on a little pointer thing that comes with the board, and it moves to the letters, spelling out what the spirit is saying. But you don't have to have the board. You can do it just as well with bits of paper with the letters on them, and a glass.»

«Und du meinst, wenn ein Geist mit uns reden will, dann bewegt sich das Glas und rutscht zu den Papierfetzen, um ein Wort zu buchstabieren?», fragte Edzard ungläubig. Er wusste nicht so recht, ob er sie auslachen sollte oder nicht. Außerdem war ihm das alles ein bisschen unheimlich.

«Exactly», Fiona confirmed.

«Und das Glas bewegt sich von alleine?»

«Yes, when you have your finger on it. You aren't allowed to push it in any direction. You just rest your finger gently on the glass and let it move along with it.»

«Und wo machen wir das?»

«Well, not here in public anyway.»

Edzard zögerte einen Moment. «Müssen wir bis Mitternacht warten, oder können wir gleich anfangen?»

«Midnight?» Fiona laughed. «We're not in a spooky film, you know. And what does that have to do with where we do it?»

«Na ja, wir können zu mir gehen, aber wenn du erst um Mitternacht kommen würdest, dann bekäme die alte Zicke von nebenan, die immer hinter mir herspioniert, sicher als Erstes einen Schlaganfall, und sofort danach würde sie ein Telegramm an meine Mutter schicken: Edzard hat Damenbesuch um Mitternacht, oder so. Und die würde glatt zurückkommen.»

Fiona found that very funny. «That's o. k.», she assured him, «we can do it now if you like. Anyway, I'm not coming as a *Dame*, but as a spiritual detective!»

Bei Edzard angekommen, fingen sie gleich an, Papier in kleinere Stücke zu schneiden, die einzelnen Buchstaben draufzuschreiben und sie auf dem Küchentisch auszubreiten.

«Und wie machen wir es mit *yes* und *no*?», fragte Edzard, «vielleicht kommt ein deutscher Geist, der kein Englisch kann.» Er grinste.

«Are you pulling my leg?» asked Fiona.

«Nee, ich dachte nur.»

«We could write JA/YES on one piece of paper and NEIN/NO on another. Would that make you happy?» She thought it was a funny idea.

«Wunschlos glücklich. Hoffentlich erwischen wir keinen Franzosen», spottete Edzard weiter. Um einem deutschen Geist entgegenzukommen, stimmte Fiona auch der Anfertigung der deutschen Buchstaben Ä, Ö, Ü und ß zu.

Fiona thought it might still be too bright for ghosts, so, after they had arranged the letters on the table and put a glass in the middle, which they had turned upside down, they closed the curtains.

Nun saßen beide da, jeder den rechten Arm ausgestreckt, Zeigefinger auf dem Glas. Sie warteten und warteten. Nichts passierte.

«Ich krieg gleich 'nen Krampf. Wie lange müssen wir noch …», fing Edzard an, aber er erhielt einen bösen Blick von Fiona; halt bloß die Klappe, bedeutete der wohl.

«Is anybody there?» Fiona said out loud. That was how her friend Helen always did it. Nothing happened. A few minutes later she repeated: «Is anybody there?» She felt the glass moving slowly.

JA / YES.

Ob Fiona das Glas geschoben hatte, fragte sich Edzard. Es war, als ob es sich von alleine bewegt hatte. Unheimlich!

«What is your name?» Fiona continued. The glass didn't move. «What is your name?» she asked again. Still nothing happened.

Nun griff Edzard ein. «Wie heißt du?» Das Glas bewegte sich langsam.

D O L L Y.

Was the ghost female? Fiona was surprised. She had only ever heard of male ghosts coming back with messages. Ghost's Lib, she thought to herself, and had to bite her lip to stop laughing.

«Du bist also ein weibliches Wesen», stellte Edzard fest. Auch er war überrascht. Wieder bewegte sich das Glas nicht. Was hatte sie bloß?

«Are you a female ghost?» Fiona tried.

JA / YES.

Fiona and Edzard grinned at each other. What language did she want to speak? Edzard fragte: «Willst du mit uns auf Deutsch reden, Dolly?»

NEIN / NO.

«Do you want to speak English to us?» Fiona asked.

NEIN / NO.

What kind of a crazy spirit had they contacted? She had answered them in both English and German but now she was saying that she didn't want to speak either of those languages. Moment mal, dachte Edzard, vielleicht meint sie, dass sie keine der beiden Sprachen ausschließlich sprechen will.

«Willst du vielleicht mal Englisch, mal Deutsch mit uns reden?», wollte er wissen.

Das Glas flitzte in Richtung JA / YES.

Die will uns verarschen, durchfuhr es Edzard. Fiona tried not to laugh. What a funny situation. Just wait till she told Helen about this! But how were they to go on now? They had contacted the spirit to try to find out something about the business with the fish barrels. Whose turn was it to ask a question? She looked at Edzard. He nodded at her.

«Dolly, do you know *Friesland Fisch* in Emden?» she enquired.

JA / YES.

Bevor Edzard die nächste Frage stellen konnte, bewegte sich das Glas von alleine weiter. Diesmal ging es zu den Buchstaben M A T J E S M M M M.

Edzard strahlte. «Ich ess die auch unheimlich gerne! Weißt du, dass in letzter Zeit da eingebrochen worden ist?»

JA / YES.

Fiona added quickly: «Do you know who it was?»

JA / YES.

«Great! Will you tell us then?»

The glass didn't move. Fiona looked at Edzard and raised her eyes up to heaven. He should try.

«Kannst du uns bitte sagen, wer es war?»

Das Glas legte los: I R E N.

«Can you tell us their names?» asked Fiona. She held her breath. This was really exciting.

The glass moved very slowly: T I R E D.

Was war das denn für ein komischer Name? Tired? Ach so! «Du bist müde?», hakte Edzard nach.

Ganz langsam schlich das Glas zum JA / YES-Papierfetzen.

Oh no, she can't go now, thought Fiona. «Dolly, could you please answer one last question before you go?» she began. «Can you tell us what these Irishmen are looking for?»

The glass started moving so slowly, it looked as if it wasn't moving at all. It made it to D, but then it stopped. They waited.

«Dolly, bist du noch da?», fragte Edzard, aber da war nichts mehr zu wollen. Dolly war weg.

«So ein Mist», fluchte Edzard, «sie hätte ja nun auch zehn Minuten später schlafen gehen können.» Er hatte völlig vergessen, dass er der Sache eine halbe Stunde zuvor noch total skeptisch gegenübergestanden hatte.

«Was that a German D or an English one?» Fiona wondered. «What could it be – drugs, maybe?»

«Oder Delphine», warf Edzard ein.

Fiona gave him a warning look. «Be serious! What begins with D? Drugs, diamonds, deadly poison …»

«Deswegen sind die Fische gestorben, was?», konnte es sich Edzard nicht verkneifen. «Oder vielleicht Daten. Eine wertvolle Datei für einen Computer? – Fisch und Mikrochips!»

«We haven't really got any further, have we?» Fiona complained.

«O doch», entgegnete Edzard, «wir haben Dolly kennen gelernt, und du weißt jetzt, wo ich wohne.»

Shining Knights

«O Mann», knurrte Edzard. Sie hatten seit dem frühen Morgen im Versteck gehockt, und nichts war passiert. Vier Tage waren inzwischen seit dem ersten Einbruch vergangen. «Was können wir bloß tun?», fragte er.

Fiona shrugged her shoulders: «I don't know, but this is boring. Nearly as boring as not chasing after imaginary fish burglars.» – «Fish burgers?», versuchte Edzard sie aufzuheitern.

«Uaah», Fiona moaned, «try a bit harder! At least if we could look down from a helicopter or from the top of one of the bridges when they're open or from anywhere high, we might get to see something.»

In Edzards Augen leuchtete es: «Gute Idee.»

«What?» Fiona didn't have a clue what he meant. «The helicopter or the bridge?»

«Nee, aber von oben. Wir können auf den Rathausturm gehen. Ich nehm das Fernglas mit.»

To get up to the *Rathausturm* you had to pay an entrance fee and go through a museum first. Pictures, models of the town, old furniture from the area and then a long hall full of flags, spears and all kinds of weapons.

«God, look at this!» Fiona exclaimed as they were passing an old brown skull full of holes.

«Tja, der hat einen mit 'nem Morgenstern auf den Kopf gekriegt», erklärte Edzard, «sieh mal, da hängt so 'n Ding.» An der Wand konnten sie gleich eine ganze Reihe dieser kugelförmigen Schlaggeräte mit langen Zacken bewundern.

«Come on, Edzard, we wanted to go up to the tower, not to hang around in a Museum», Fiona said impatiently.

«Ej, langsam, guck mal hier», Edzard hielt sie zurück und zeigte auf ein Bild. Ein Mann in Rüstung, mit schräg aufgesetztem Hut, Lanze, spitzer Nase und stechenden Augen. «Edzard der Große. Graf von Ostfriesland. Geboren 1463, gestorben 1528», las Edzard vor. «Mein großer Vorgänger.»

«Big deal», said Fiona, «then go *vor*, you *großer Vorgänger*, otherwise we'll never make it to the top.»

They turned left into another part of the hall. Now it was Fiona who got excited. She couldn't believe her eyes. In front of her was a whole gallery of shining knights in armour. All lined up, ready for battle.

«Ja, siehste, unsere Rüstkammer ist nicht umsonst so berühmt», freute sich Edzard, als er ihr plötzliches Interesse bemerkte. «Das hier sind Harnische, das sind Beinpanzer und das Brustpanzer», erklärte er. «Hier, der ist von 1570. Eine irre Reihe, was? So, ich bin jetzt Edzard der Zweitgrößte und du die Königin von England.»

«You must be joking! Queen of England?» protested Fiona. «If I have to be a Queen, then I'll be Queen Maeve of Connaught.»

«Von mir aus, Queen Maeve. Also, präsentiert die Morgensterne! Fertig zur Parade!», rief er.

They marched along the row of lovely old polished suits of armour. Fiona counted twenty-six altogether, some in shining silver, some in black and silver. It really looks great, she thought. Why don't the men try to steal something from here instead of rooting around in barrels of stinking fish? It would be great fun to chase a thief in old armour through the streets of Emden.

«And now, back again», she commanded, «knights of the Frisian moors, prepare to attack the Irish fish mafia!»

«Bist du verrückt?», entfuhr es Edzard. «Wenn uns jemand hört!»

«All right, all right», Fiona stopped their game, «there's no need to be paranoid about it. Maybe we should move on, though. After all, it is serious detective work we're into and not fun and games in a Museum, isn't it?»

Edzard wusste nicht genau, ob sie ihn jetzt auf den Arm nehmen wollte oder nicht, und sagte lieber nichts. Weiter ging es durch einen Raum mit langen Gewehren und Munition und dann eine Wendeltreppe hoch zum Turm.

It was quite windy up at the top. Fiona was amazed at how

much green she could see from there. Directly below them she saw the Hafenrundfahrtsboot pulling out from the dock. The Delft was pretty much dominated by the red ship *Deutsche Bucht.* Fiona took her camera out of her pocket.

«Willst du jetzt einen auf richtige Touristin machen, oder was?», spottete Edzard.

«Oh shut up», she replied. «I want to have something to show my friends when I go back. Emden looks great from up here!» She took a few photos.

«So, wollen wir mal sehen, ob man unser Fahndungsobjekt von hier aus erkennen kann.» Edzard zog sie weiter.

«Hey! Isn't that the woman who you thought wanted to buy Matjes the other day?» It had just slipped out before Fiona knew what she was saying.

«I beg your pardon?» said the woman, looking cooly at the two of them.

«Excuse me», Fiona said quickly, «we were passing by a kiosk the other day and heard a woman asking for matches. My friend here thought she wanted Matjes, and wondered why anyone would try to buy fish at a newspaper kiosk.»

«I see», said the woman slowly, «that could have been me all right.» She looked at Fiona and said: «You sound Irish to me.»

«Yes, I'm from Dublin», Fiona answered.

«And I'm from Donegal», the woman said. «What are the two of you up to at the moment?» she asked.

«Nothing in particular», Fiona pretended.

«Well, can I treat you to an ice-cream, then? We Irish abroad have to stick together after all, *an ea*?» – «*Sea!*» Fiona grinned.

«That was Irish», she explained to Edzard, «it means *isn't that right* and *yes, it is!*»

Sie gingen in die Eisdiele, in der Edzard und Fiona sich getroffen hatten. Die nächste halbe Stunde langweilte Edzard sich ziemlich: Die beiden redeten über Schulen, die von Nonnen geleitet werden, und von lauter Sachen, von denen er keine Ahnung hatte. Außerdem redeten sie so schnell, dass er ohnehin kaum etwas verstand. Fiona aber schien die Frau zu mögen.

«By the way», the woman asked, «what exactly are Matjes?»
Fiona looked at Edzard. Er versuchte eine Erklärung: «Well,
it's some kind of herring. It's a Dutch word. Don't you call
them Matjes in English, too?»

«Could they be what we call young herring?», fragte die Frau.

«Maybe», stimmte Edzard ihr zu, «Matjes are young.»

Die Frau schien einen Moment nachzudenken. Sie sah die
beiden an. «Well, I think I'll be off now. Maybe we'll meet again
sometime», sagte sie dann.

«Hoffentlich nicht», stöhnte Edzard, als sie wieder allein waren, «ist dir was aufgefallen?»

«Oh God, here we go again», sighed Fiona, «just because
she's Irish and mentioned Matjes, you probably think she's
going to break into the fish place as well now, am I right?»

«Na, ich weiß nicht, so wie sie dich ausgefragt hat und deinen
Fragen über sie ausgewichen ist …»

«What do you mean?» Fiona was starting to get annoyed.

«Na ja, alles, was wir jetzt von ihr wissen, ist, dass sie Mary
Murphy heißt, in einer Versicherungsgesellschaft arbeitet und
hier Urlaub macht. Und du, du hast ihr immer brav geantwor-
tet.»

«Rubbish! I didn't tell her about our fish burglars, for
example.»

«Das fehlte auch noch. Ich weiß nicht, ich traue ihr nicht. Sie
ist regelrecht zusammengezuckt, als du auf dem Turm das Wort
Matjes gesagt hast. Und später schien sie nicht mal zu wissen,
was Matjes sind. Sehr verdächtig.»

«Oh come on, Edzard, no matter who we meet, you think
they must have something to do with your big case. You know
what you need, Mr. Sherlock Holmes? You need your head
examined.»

Edzard wurde wütend. «Sei doch nicht so aggressiv. Ich sag ja
nicht, dass sie Fische klauen will oder so. Aber eins ist sicher:
Als wir sie da oben auf dem Turm überrascht haben, war ihr
Fernglas genau in Richtung *Friesland Fisch* gerichtet!»

«That's it», Fiona said quietly but firmly, «you are totally paranoid. There are only four sides at the top of the *Rathaus-turm* which you can look from. The chances that she would be looking in that direction when we saw her were one to four. For God's sake, you think that everyone in the world wants to steal your beloved Matjes. Crazy, just crazy. Well, let me tell you this: You can phone me whenever you've solved your case, Mr. Holmes, but till then, good-bye and enjoy your bloody fish!»

Das Dunkel lichtet sich

Die blöde Ziege, dachte Edzard, als er am nächsten Tag zum Versteck lief. So eine blöde Kuh! Und wahrscheinlich hatte sie ihn mit dem Geist auch bloß veräppelt und die ganze Zeit das Glas geschoben. Dolly! Pah! Als wenn Geister Dolly hießen! Aber er würde es ihr schon beweisen. Typisch Mädchen, bloß weil es mal nicht auf Anhieb klappt, gleich alles hinzuschmeißen.

Good that Dad has time for breakfast at home today, Fiona thought while she poured the tea. Chatting to him would take her mind off things. She kept thinking about that silly Edzard. Typical fellow! Always wanting to play cowboys and Indians.

Edzard war kaum im Versteck, als er sah, wie sich von der Brücke her ein Mann näherte. Er traute seinen Augen kaum. Über die Schienen gelaufen kam ein eleganter schwarzhaariger Mann, eindeutig – das war der Typ, der am Sonntag den ersten Einbruch begangen hatte, den Fiona am Telefon belauscht hatte, der sie um Kleingeld gebeten hatte. Edzard stockte der Atem. Der Mann kam direkt auf den Einstieg ins Versteck zu.

«Serves them right», said Mr. Burke to his daughter, putting the *Irish Times* down on the table. «What serves who right?» Fiona wanted to know. «The Tiffens. You know, the big business family in Dublin. They're always in the paper because of some marvellous piece of art or jewelry or something which he bought for his wife. Too much money altogether. They don't know what to do with it. Anyone could have said that they'd be broken into sooner or later.»

Edzard zog sich schnell hinter einen Haufen aus Müll und Autoreifen zurück. Der Mann sah in das Versteck hinein, blickte zurück übers Wasser in Richtung *Friesland Fisch*, schaute noch einmal nach links und rechts und kletterte dann schnell durch den Einstieg. Mist! Edzards Herz klopfte. Wie konnte er bloß unentdeckt bleiben? Der Schwarzhaarige blickte sich aber gar nicht um, sondern holte ein kleines Opernglas hervor, zündete sich eine Zigarette an und begann, das Gebäude der Fischfabrik zu beobachten.

Fiona picked up the paper and began to read.

Further Developments in Tiffen Case

A Garda spokesman has confirmed that no trace has yet been found of the jewelry stolen from the Tiffen's residence, ‹Salomo›, earlier this month. As we reported at the time, the missing pieces include the famous ‹Dresden Diamond›, a 41-carat green teardrop-shaped stone of inestimable value, which originally came from India. Among its previous owners was August the Second (also known as August the Strong), King of Poland (1670–1733).
Police followed a trail to Co. Waterford, which ended at the harbour in Dunmore East. They sus-

pect that the jewels may have been smuggled out of the country. Dunmore East is one of the major fish and beef exporting harbours in Ireland. The main destinations are America, Japan and Germany.

Fiona whistled softly under her breath.

Bevor Edzard noch einen klaren Gedanken fassen und überlegen konnte, wie er in dieser Lage unentdeckt bleiben könnte, erhielt die Situation im Versteck eine überraschende Wende.

«Jesus Christ, it's the bloody bastard himself!», fluchte der Mann plötzlich, steckte das Opernglas weg, nahm noch einen tiefen Zug aus der Zigarette und trat sie dann aus. Er wirkte unheimlich angespannt.

Fiona felt her hands getting cold and clammy. She put the newspaper down. Stolen jewelry, fish export, destination Germany, all those Irish people turning up in Emden all of a sudden. Jewelry. Diamonds. D. D for the ‹Dresden Diamond›? Was that what Dolly was going to tell them?

«Dad», she said, «Dad ...»

«Yeah?»

«I have to go now. I've just remembered that I'd arranged to meet someone in town.»

«Oh, is it that Hilke girl? I never asked how you got on with her.»

For a moment Fiona wondered if she should tell her father everything. But would he believe her? Diamonds in smelly fish? She found it hard to imagine herself. And even if he did believe her, it would take too long to explain. Maybe some other time. Now she had to find Edzard. Quickly.

«Ah ... yes, Hilke», she said, giving him a kiss good-bye, «and I'm late already. You know the way these Germans are, always on time.»

Der Schwarzhaarige drückte sich gegen die Mauer neben dem Einstieg ins Versteck. Kommt da etwa noch jemand?, fragte sich Edzard. Er hätte zu gern gewusst, was draußen vorging. Nach einer halben Minute – sie kam ihm vor wie eine halbe Ewigkeit – war er schlauer. Am Wasser entlang schlenderte, Hände in den Taschen, der Typ aus dem grünen Auto, Freddy. Edzard hätte fast gelacht. Eine echte Vollversammlung. Und Fiona hatte vorausgesagt, dass er im Versteck sitzen und verschimmeln würde! Freddy blieb am Wasser stehen, schaute zur Fischfabrik, blickte betont unauffällig nach links und nach rechts, drehte sich um und kam langsam, aber direkt auf den Einstieg ins Versteck zu.

Fiona raced along on her bike. Keep cool, Fiona, she told herself, just because someone stole some jewelry in Ireland and because there are a few suspicious Irish people in Emden doesn't necessarily mean that the two things have anything to do with each other. Keep your cool! But as much as she tried to calm herself down, it just didn't work. She raced through the streets feeling very excited. A little voice in her head asked her if it was because she was glad that she had found a pretext to meet Edzard again. Of course not, she answered it angrily, this is a purely criminal affair, and all I'm doing is bringing along some important new information.

Freddy war direkt vor dem Versteck angekommen. Langsam steckte er den Kopf hinein.
«Take that, you fucking bastard!» Mit einer unglaublichen Geschwindigkeit hatte der Schwarzhaarige ihm einen Kinnhaken versetzt und war aus dem Versteck herausgesprungen. Edzard hielt es nicht mehr hinter seiner Deckung aus, er schlich zum Einstieg. Draußen packte der Schwarzhaarige Freddy gerade am Kragen. «You bloody double-crosser!» Er verpasste ihm noch einen. Der Überraschungsangriff schien Freddy völlig außer Fassung gebracht zu haben, er leistete kaum Widerstand. Der Schwarzhaarige stieß ihm das Knie in den Magen, versetzte

ihm einen Handkantenschlag in den Nacken und schmiss ihn ins Wasser.

Edzard kam sich vor wie im Kino. Als Nächstes würde wahrscheinlich Kojak mit Blaulicht vorfahren. All das schien höchst unwirklich. «Help!», schrie Freddy im Wasser zappelnd. Der Schwarzhaarige drehte sich um und rannte weg. Und nun, dachte Edzard, was mach ich nun? Im Fernsehen kam an so einer Stelle immer ein Schnitt, und man sah was anderes.

Fiona had just reached the corner of the street, which led to the hiding-place when she saw a man running towards her. He changed his pace into a brisk walk, and turned right into the next street. Wasn't that the fellow who she had listened to on the phone, who had asked them for change for the cigarette machine? Had something just happened? Fionas first impulse was to go to the hide-out to see if Edzard was there, and if he was still o.k. But then, she thought, maybe keeping an eye on this fellow was an ideal opportunity to find out a bit more. She turned left and followed the man from a safe distance.

Edzard war kaum aus dem Versteck geklettert, als schon drei Hafenarbeiter auf den Hilferuf angerannt kamen.

«Der hätte lieber schwimmen als Englisch lernen sollen», kalauerte der eine, während er dem Mann im Wasser ein Seil zuwarf. Edzard blieb im Hintergrund; er mochte auf keinen Fall mit der Sache in Verbindung gebracht werden, jetzt, wo endlich Bewegung hineinzukommen schien.

«Thank you very much», bedankte sich Freddy, als er wieder an Land war. Also kein Deutscher, registrierte Edzard.

«I was walking too close to the edge and I must have slipped. Thanks again.»

Aha, dachte Edzard, ausgerutscht. So, so. Freddy lehnte auch das Angebot ab, ins Büro der Holzhandelsfirma zu gehen und sich abzutrocknen: «No thanks, my car is parked over there. I'll make it home all right», sagte er und lief davon.

The black-haired man kept going until he came to a phone-box. There were two phone-boxes side by side, and he disappeared into one of them. I'd love to know what he's saying now, thought Fiona. Should she risk it? She went into the other box and dialled Edzard's number. Maybe he was at home after all. Wouldn't it be brilliant if she could give him a simultaneous translation into German of what the man was saying in the next box? She turned her back to the man – there were only two panes of glass separating them – and tried to listen. Fortunately the man was very excited and was almost screaming. «Of course it's not good that he knows we're here … Yes, I know! … But still, he bloody well deserved it!»

Edzard didn't answer the phone, so Fiona had to invent a phone-call. She nearly started talking in English, but just stopped herself in time. «Ja, hallo, das ist Herr Weiß. Er wohnt in München. Wer ist das? Das ist Fräulein Heim. Sie wohnt in Köln», she said into the phone. Those were the first lines of her German textbook at school. The teacher had made her class learn them off by heart. Funny how stupid things like that can come in handy, she thought.

The black-haired fellow put down the receiver, left the phone-box and then stopped. Fiona heard the blood pumping in her ears. «O du fröhliche, o du selige, gnadenbringende Weihnachtszeit», she continued. That was the refrain of a Christmas carol they had sung in school. Not very appropriate for this time of year, she thought, but at least it was German.

The fellow looked at her. For far too long, she thought. He was really staring at her now. Her mind went blank. She couldn't think of anything else she could say in German. «Ja, ja», she repeated a few times as if responding to someone. Oh God, he was probably going to open the door any minute now and attack her. «Ja, ja», she said once more.

When she dared to look out again, she saw him walking away down the street. But she didn't feel like following him any further now. She listened to the phone ringing at the other end. Edzard definitely wasn't at home.

Edzard wusste nicht so recht weiter. Jetzt im Versteck zu bleiben war wohl sinnlos. Er schlenderte zur nächsten Telefonzelle und rief Fiona an. Wahrscheinlich würde sie ihm nicht mal glauben. Aber erzählen musste er ihr schon, was passiert war. Oder suchte er nur einen Vorwand, um sie wieder zu treffen? Edzard wies das weit von sich. Doch so rein aus detektivischen Gründen musste sie natürlich auf dem Laufenden gehalten werden. Er ließ es klingeln und klingeln. Keine Antwort. Die ist bestimmt an den Deich gefahren und sonnt sich, knurrte er in Gedanken. Und nun? Einfach ein bisschen rumlaufen. Erst nach einer Weile merkte er, dass seine Füße ihn zielstrebig zu *ihrer* Eisdiele führten.

And now what? Fiona didn't really feel like it, but she knew it had to be done. God only knows what had happened there. Was it Edzard that the black-haired fellow had been talking about? It wasn't very likely. It probably had something to do with that other fellow who she and Edzard thought was called Freddy. She took all her courage into her hands and looked into the hide-out. «Edzard?» she called. There was no reply. She went to the next phone-box and dialled his number again. There was still no reply. She didn't know what to do now. She cycled around for a bit. After a while she noticed that her cycling around looked more like a cycling straight, and that she was riding straight towards her and Edzard's ice-cream parlour.

Bestandsaufnahme

When Fiona got to the ice-cream parlour, she saw Edzard sitting at a table sipping a milk-shake. She wasn't really surprised. «Fancy meeting you here», she said as cooly as she could, «have you been waiting long?»

«Hallo, Fiona! Nee, gerade erst gekommen», antwortete Edzard möglichst beiläufig. Dabei war er schon beim zweiten Milkshake und hatte überlegt, ob er wieder gehen sollte. Einen Moment trafen sich ihre Blicke.

«You wouldn't believe what I …»

«Du glaubst mir bestimmt nicht, was vorhin …», platzte es dann gleichzeitig aus beiden heraus. Sie hielten inne und lachten. «Also, ladies first», entschied Edzard großmütig, obwohl er der Meinung war, dass er auf jeden Fall das Spannendere zu erzählen hatte.

Fiona told Edzard about the newspaper article, the black-haired fellow, the phone-call, and the frightening way he had stared at her. Edzard berichtete vom unglaublichen Massenandrang im Versteck, von der Klopperei und davon, dass Freddy, wenn der Blonde wirklich so hieß, auch jemand war, der Englisch sprach, vielleicht sogar noch ein Ire. Unterbrochen von vielen Ooooh!, Aaaah!, Das hältste ja im Kopf nicht aus! und That's just unbelievable!, rekonstruierten sie den bisherigen Ablauf des Tages.

«Na, und glaubst du mir nun, dass da was faul ist?», fragte Edzard herausfordernd.

«Oh yes», Fiona admitted, «the question is, do you think it has anything to do with the robbery in Ireland?»

«Kann gut sein.»

«But what?» Fiona still wasn't sure.

«O. k. In der Zeitung steht, die Spur verliert sich in Dunmore East oder wie der Hafen da heißt …»

«Yeah.»

«Na ja, dann könnten die Gangster doch die Juwelen mit dem Fisch geschmuggelt haben», vermutete Edzard.

«And Herr Janssen told me that the barrels are always on the pier for a while. Unprotected», Fiona added, «but can you think of any reason why anyone would put such a beautiful diamond and other jewels into a barrel full of stinking fish?» she persisted.

«Erstens stinkt Fisch nicht, wenn er frisch ist, aber davon abgesehen kann ich mir das auch nicht erklären. Es sei denn ...», er überlegte einen Moment, «es sei denn, jemand wurde verfolgt und musste sie in letzter Minute irgendwie loswerden.»

«Yes, but there was no talk of a chase in the paper», Fiona reminded him.

«Stimmt, also nichts Genaues weiß man nicht.»

«It doesn't really matter. Let's assume for a moment it was like that. The jewels are in with the fish, right? Then they're transported in a container to Emden. In a sealed container.»

«Und solange der Container zu ist, kommt man schlecht ran», zog Edzard die Konsequenz. «Also ist hier die erste Gelegenheit, um sich die Dinger wieder untern Nagel zu reißen.»

«Um what?» Fiona was lost.

«Um sie wieder in Besitz zu nehmen.»

«Yes, but why the two burglaries?» she asked, puzzled.

«Offensichtlich sind das Feinde», versuchte Edzard eine Erklärung.

«Or else they worked together at the beginning and then one of them double-crossed the other.»

«Doppelkreuz?» Jetzt wusste Edzard nicht weiter.

«Tricked», Fiona tried.

«Betrügen. O ja, haben wir auch so ähnlich: Aufs Kreuz legen. Moment mal», fiel es Edzard wieder ein, «ich glaub, der Schwarzhaarige hat sogar so was Ähnliches gesagt, als er Freddy einen verpasst hat.»

«That's interesting», said Fiona, «now what do we know so far? There is the elegant black-haired fellow. He is obviously working with someone else who we don't know yet – whoever it is he keeps phoning.»

«Der geheimnisvolle Mr. X», unterbrach Edzard sie.

«Or Ms. X, we can't say yet.»

Edzard schüttelte den Kopf: «Glaub ich nicht. So was ist Männersache.»

Well, in this case I don't mind if it is purely Männersache, Fiona thought, even though she didn't agree with Edzard's generalization. It was bad enough as it was. If Freddy was Irish as well now, then all the baddies were Irish so far. She hoped that at least Mr. X would be a German.

«O. k.», she said, «Mr. X and the black-haired fellow are working against Freddy with the green Golf.»

Wieder unterbrach Edzard: «Gegen den Typen im grünen Golf, von dem wir annehmen, dass er Freddy heißt», korrigierte er.

«Oh God, Edzard, if he isn't Freddy, who is? There can't be an army of people involved.» Fiona sighed.

«Gut. Also nehmen wir an, dass das Freddy ist. Und der Schwarzhaarige wusste seit ein paar Tagen, dass Freddy in Emden ist, denn er hatte sich ja gleich versteckt, als er ihn gesehen hatte», fuhr Edzard mit der Bestandsaufnahme fort.

«It's all so complicated», Fiona moaned, «anyway, Freddy knows that the black-haired fellow is here, too, because he was beaten up and thrown into the water by him.»

«Und alle sind noch hier, weil die Diamanten offensichtlich noch nicht eingetroffen sind. Vielleicht warten sie auf den nächsten Container. Dabei fällt mir was ein: Als du heute das Telefongespräch belauscht hast, war das ein Orts- oder ein Ferngespräch? Ich meine, hat er Geld nachgeworfen?»

Fiona thought for a moment and then shrugged her shoulders: «I can't remember. I tried to look at him as little as possible. And I was too scared to notice much anyway.»

«Also wissen wir nicht, ob Mr. X schon da ist oder nicht. Kannst du dich noch an das andere Telefongespräch erinnern, das in der Kneipe?»

«Yeah.»

«Hattest du da nicht gehört, dass Mr. X hierher kommen sollte?»

«Yeah.»

«Und hast du unseren Mr. X bisher irgendwo mal in *action* gesehen?»

«No», Fiona sighed, «but we don't know who he is or what he looks like. And would you ever stop this awful detective question and answer routine! What do you have in mind?»

«Erinnerst du dich … o. k., keine Fragen mehr», unterbrach Edzard sich, «aber als du so getan hast, als ob du Informationen für dein Projekt sammeln wolltest, hast du da nicht gehört, dass dieser Geschäftspartner am Freitag kommen wollte? Und was ist heute? Freitag! Und wen haben wir bis heute noch nicht gesehen? – Mr. X! Verdächtig, nicht?»

Fiona felt exhausted. All these complications. She had thought it was completely normal for two business colleagues to meet each other, but then these days nothing seemed to be normal any more.

«Wollen wir nicht in Richtung *Friesland Fisch* radeln und schauen, ob der Geschäftsfreund schon eingetroffen ist», schlug Edzard vor, «oder fällt dir was Besseres ein?»

Fiona couldn't think of anything better. In fact, she could hardly think at all. Weren't holidays supposed to be relaxing? Well, at least she couldn't say she found it boring in Emden any more. «I'm hungry», she said.

«O. k., dann ziehen wir uns erst mal 'ne Currywurst rein», meinte Edzard, «und dann ab in Richtung Hafen.»

Fiona didn't know what a *Currywurst* was, but she didn't have the energy to ask. They paid for their milk-shakes and left.

More Phone Calls

«Ein toller Kahn, was?», sagte Edzard und zeigte auf ein etwa zwölf Meter langes Boot, das am Ufer vertäut war. «*Wassergeist*, der lag hier noch nie.»

«I wonder is it a relation of Dolly's?» Fiona joked. «Just look inside. It's all done in wood. Gorgeous!»

They stood there for a while admiring it. «If I were you with your detective's suspicions, I would think it was very odd that a boat, which wasn't here before is now parked within walking distance from *Friesland Fisch*. It would be a good hiding-place and a great way to escape», Fiona teased Edzard.

Der nahm sie ernst: «Versteck ja – auf jeden Fall besser als unseres da drüben auf der anderen Seite. Aber Fluchtfahrzeug? Bei einem Boot dieser Größe müssen die Brücken hochgeklappt werden, und das passiert nur zu festgelegten Zeiten. Außerdem, selbst wenn es zeitlich hinhaut, dann würden die in der Seeschleuse aufgehalten. Eigentlich schade, 'ne Verfolgungsjagd mit dem Boot, das wär doch was!»

Fiona smiled. Typical Edzard! «And what now?» she asked, «I can hardly go up to Herr Janssen and ask whether the business associate who may have smuggled diamonds in the barrels has arrived yet, and you can't go near the place either, because he thinks you've thrown his fish around and wants to put you *kopfüber in ein Fass mit Salzwasser.*»

Sie überlegten eine Weile. «Hast du deine Pocketkamera bei dir?», fragte Edzard plötzlich. «Dann könntest du nämlich hingehen und einfach sagen, für dein Projekt brauchst du noch ein paar Fotos. Und ich setze mich hier auf die Bank und bewache so lange den *Wassergeist.* Vielleicht rückt der ja die Gläser auf dem Tisch im Boot und löst alle unsere Rätsel.»

When Fiona cycled around the corner she saw lots of barrels, stacked on pallets, being brought into the plant. Herr Janssen was standing there with a rather stout man in a leather jacket. Both of them had their backs to Fiona and were talking.

«... this evening», she heard the man saying, and Herr Janssen's reply: «O. k. We'll have to put it in an extra shift tomorrow to get the processing going.»

«Hello, Herr Janssen», Fiona interrupted them. Herr Janssen looked startled. «I interviewed you for my school project, remember?» Fiona reminded him. «‹What happens to an Irish herring before it ends up on a German dinner table.› I was wondering if I could take some pictures to round it all off nicely.»

«Natürlich, of course», replied Herr Janssen, «Fianna, wasn't that your name?»

«Fiona», she corrected.

«Well, Fiona», he continued, «this is a fellow countryman of yours, Mr. O'Donnell. He is my business associate from Waterford.» Fiona smiled at him.

«Nice to meet you, Mr. O'Donnell. Maybe I could take a picture of the two of you together for my project. ‹The Irish exporter and his German business associate›. That would be nice.»

She pulled out her camera and was ready to take the picture when Mr. O'Donnell stopped her rudely: «What happens to an Irish herring in Germany, my foot! School projects, what a load of rubbish. You should be practicing your spelling or your writing and not wasting our precious time.» He turned to Herr Janssen. «You were telling me about some young lad who was throwing your fish around the place. She should do her project on him: find out who throws good Irish herring around German warehouses. Kids these days, really! School projects! They don't learn anything proper any more.»

Fiona was flabbergasted. Why was he so angry with her? Was he trying to hide something? Why didn't he want to have his photo taken? She looked at Herr Janssen, but he just said:

«Maybe some other time, Fianna, we are very busy at the moment.» Fiona got on her bike and cycled away. As she was leaving, she heard Herr Janssen's secretary calling: «Mr. O'Donnell, Telefon!»

When she got to the bench beside the boat there was no Edzard to be seen. Oh God, she thought, I hope he's not starting to play hide and seek with me now. She waited a while, but there was still no sign of him. Ice-cream parlour again, I suppose, she said to herself.

«Gott sei Dank, dass du da bist!» Edzard empfing sie diesmal *vor* der Eisdiele. «Ich habe in letzter Zeit so viel Eis gegessen, mir ist der Appetit drauf vergangen», entschuldigte er sich.

Before Fiona could say a word, he started to tell her what had happened.

Er hatte auf einer Bank gesessen, nur ein paar Meter weg vom

Boot. Plötzlich war jemand aus der Kajüte heraus an Deck gekommen. Nicht einfach irgendjemand, sondern der Schwarzhaarige. Als er Edzard sah, schaute er ihn lange prüfend an, jedenfalls hatte Edzard diesen Eindruck gehabt.

«Do you mean to say he was down there in the boat the whole time?» Fiona interrupted him.

Edzard nickte.

«And ...», she paused, «... does that mean he heard everything we said when we were standing in front of it?»

«Könnte sein», antwortete Edzard leicht resigniert, «ist sogar wahrscheinlich. Als er wieder runtergegangen ist, hab ich mich verdünnisiert. Aber nur bis zur nächsten Querstraße, da hab ich mich versteckt. Er ist ziemlich bald wieder rausgekommen und weggegangen. Ich mit gehörigem Abstand hinterher. Du musst dann wohl zurückgekommen sein, als wir gerade weg waren. Also, du wirst es nicht glauben, er ist wieder telefonieren gegangen. Ich hab mich von hinten rangeschlichen, an die Seite von der Telefonzelle, durch die man nicht durchsehen kann. Ich habe ganz schön Angst gehabt. Man versteht da auch kaum was.»

«And did you hear anything at all?» Fiona was really curious.

«Vielleicht bilde ich mir das nur ein, aber ich glaube, er hat so was gesagt wie *a boy and a girl watching me* und dann *o. k., so you'll look after that.* Aber wie gesagt, es kann sein, dass ich mir das nur einbilde.»

This time Fiona didn't think that Edzard was just imagining things. «Well, if you just think for a minute: he noticed someone running away when he was in the fish plant, he saw me listening to him in the phone-box, he probably heard the two of us talking in front of the boat, and then he saw you sitting there beside it. That's more than enough to make anyone suspicious. So, if you've got it right, the mysterious Mr. X is going to *look after* us.»

«Tolle Aussichten», versuchte Edzard zu scherzen, «da lernen wir ihn endlich kennen.» Ganz wohl war ihm nicht dabei. Then Fiona told him what had happened to her. «Oh God», she said when she was just finished, «I've just remembered something. As I was cycling away, Mr. O'Donnell was called to the phone. You don't think …»

«… dass Mr. O'Donnell Mr. X ist? Es sieht jetzt sehr danach aus. Oder glaubst du immer noch, dass er ein unschuldiger Geschäftsmann ist?»

Fiona had to admit that it was all very odd.

«Also», Edzard war aufgeregt, «wir können auf heute Abend oder heute Nacht gespannt sein. Wenn die morgen die Lieferung Fisch verarbeiten wollen, muss heute Nacht etwas geschehen. Da wird's *action* geben!»

«I thought this morning was action enough», Fiona sighed, «and what are we going to do till tonight?»

«Abwarten und Tee trinken», sagte Edzard, «oder noch besser, abwarten und was essen. Ich hab immer noch Hunger. Ich kauf mir 'n paar Matjes.»

«And I'll buy some *pommern,* or whatever it is, you call chips here. Even though you don't do them at all properly. There's never any vinegar on them.»

Edzard verzog das Gesicht. «Essig. Brrr. Mayo oder Ketchup ja, aber bitte keinen Essig. Außerdem heißen die *Pommes* und nicht *Pommern.*»

«*Pommes,* then», Fiona muttered, «come on, let's go for our fish 'n' chips.»

The Mysterious Mary Murphy

«Do you know something, Edzard?» Fiona said.

«Hmmm?», kam es zurück. Edzard verschlang gerade einen halben Matjes.

«The one thing that's really awful about this whole affair?»

«Hmmm?» Edzards Hauptinteresse schien eher bei seinem Fisch zu liegen.

Fiona kept going regardless. «That Emden seems to be full of so many horrible Irish people all of a sudden. Had you ever met an Irish people before?» she demanded.

Edzard schüttelte den Kopf und brachte immerhin ein klares «Nee» zustande. Ein Kunststück bei vollem Mund.

Fiona had finished her chips. She threw the cardboard plate away. «God only knows what you think of us. We aren't really a nation of thieves and double-crossers and nasty businessmen, you know», she tried to convince him.

Edzard schluckte den letzten Bissen runter. «Ach, wirklich nicht? Also meiner Meinung nach ist das typisch irisch. Von wegen rotes Haar und Sommersprossen! Schlitzaugen, äh Schlitzohren, Verbrecher und Prügler, das seid ihr. Von dir abgesehen natürlich. Aber du weißt ja: Die Ausnahme bestätigt die Regel.» Er klang ernst.

Fiona was quite upset. «We aren't at all like that. You should come over sometime and see for yourself that lots of Irish people really are nice and friendly. Unless the country has gone completely to hell since I left a couple of weeks ago, that is.» She looked worried.

Edzard gelang es weiterhin, ein bedenkliches Gesicht zu machen. «Na gut, vielleicht besuch ich dich mal, aber nur, wenn ich eine kugelsichere Weste tragen darf.»

Fiona was trying to think of a smart reply, when she saw a familiar figure approaching them. «Oh look, there's Mary Murphy!» she exclaimed.

«Und zu welcher Sorte Iren gehört die?», fragte Edzard. Dabei stand für ihn die Antwort eigentlich schon fest: Er mochte sie nicht besonders. Fiona didn't have time to answer him. Mary Murphy had reached their bench. «Hello, Mary», she said.

«Hello, Fiona, hello, Edward. What are you two up to?» Mary asked.

Edzard antwortete schnell: «Nothing much, and you?»

Mary Murphy sah ihn leicht verwirrt an. «Nothing much either. You know the usual things you do when you're on holidays – go for walks, sunbathe, swim, eat ice-cream. Would you like to join me for one now?» Wieder übernahm Edzard die Antwort: «No! ... thank you. We have eaten so much ice-cream in the last time that we place.» Mary didn't know what he meant. «What he wants to say is that we're going to burst if we eat any more ice-cream», Fiona explained. She gave Edzard a dirty look before continuing: «But we could join you for a cup of coffee somewhere.»

Auch das noch, dachte Edzard verärgert. Warum konnte sie sie nicht abwimmeln? Nun mussten sie mit dieser Frau rumhängen. Dabei hätte er viel lieber mit Fiona überlegt, wie sie am Abend vorgehen sollten.

Edzard wollte diesmal etwas mehr über Mary Murphy herausbekommen. Sie sollte sie nicht wieder so einfach ausfragen können. Wieso war sie auf Emden als Ferienziel gekommen, wollte er von ihr wissen.

«Oh, I just wanted to come to Germany», she said, «and I wanted to be by the sea.» Edzard fand das komisch. Die meisten Touristen in Emden waren auf der Durchreise zu den Ostfriesischen Inseln. Die wenigsten blieben direkt in der Stadt. Und warum kam sie nach Deutschland, wenn sie kein Deutsch sprach, bohrte er weiter. Mary Murphy was annoyed: «Maybe you'll want to visit China some day and you will hardly learn Chinese just for that occasion, will you?» She turned to Fiona and started talking to her instead.

Ganz schön clever ist die, dachte Edzard, die lässt sich nicht so ohne weiteres ausfragen. Jetzt erzählte sie Fiona gerade, sie hätte seit ihrer Ankunft in Emden keine Zeitung mehr gelesen. Ob man hier irgendwo eine *Irish Times* kaufen könne?

«I don't know», Fiona answered, «we get our Saturday's edition sent directly to us.»

«And has anything exciting happened recently?»

Fiona thought for a moment. She looked at Edzard. Der nickte unauffällig. «Do you know the Tiffens?» she asked Mary. Täuschte sich Edzard, oder war Mary da nicht unwillkürlich zusammengezuckt. «Well, not personally», she said, «but everyone has heard of them. Why?»

Fiona berichtete, was in der Zeitung gestanden hatte. Als sie von dem Verdacht sprach, dass die Juwelen ins Ausland geschmuggelt worden seien, beobachtete Edzard die Frau ganz genau. «And what do you think about it? Where do you think the jewels are?» Mary asked, looking at the two of them intently.

«Woher sollen denn ausgerechnet wir das wissen?», fragte Edzard – das sollte ein Signal an Fiona sein, dass sie einen auf *Wirwissenvonnix* machen sollte.

Mary didn't understand what Edzard had said. «He just asked how *we* should know», Fiona translated. «Well you seem to be pretty interested in the whole affair. Otherwise you'd hardly remember all the details, would you?» Mary persisted.

«Oh well, we have our suspicions», Fiona said cooly, «we've noticed some fairly strange things happening here lately.»

Idiotin, schimpfte Edzard in Gedanken, warum erzählst du ihr das?

Einen Moment lang trafen sich drei Blicke, ein wütender von Edzard, ein herausfordernder von Fiona und ein nachdenklicher von Mary. Eine dieser ewigen Sekunden lang sagte keiner etwas. Dann rückte Mary näher an die beiden heran: «Look, I feel I can trust you two. Edward kept asking me questions about why I was on holidays here. He found it odd. Well, he is right, I'm not here on holidays. As I told you, I work for an insurance company in Ireland. That part of my story was true. But I don't work in an office there – I'm a detective.»

Edzard und Fiona sahen sich groß an. Stimmte das? Gab es überhaupt weibliche Detektive?

«Now, my insurance company», Mary continued, «is the one which is going to have to cough up the money if the Tiffen's jewels aren't found, so I've been put on the case. The trail has led me to Emden.»

Fiona stared at Mary. «Amazing!» she exclaimed.

Mary went on. «Of course if, as you say, you have noticed strange things happening here over the past few days, I'd be very grateful if you could tell me about them.»

«Well …» Fiona began. Edzard unterbrach sie sofort. Diese angebliche Detektivin sollte es nicht so leicht haben. Erst mal musste sie beweisen, dass sie überhaupt eine war.

«What do *you* know so far?», gab er zurück. Diese Frage schien ihr nicht besonders zu gefallen, aber sie versuchte, es nicht zu zeigen.

She took a deep breath. «It seems that the jewels were smuggled out of the country – just like you said. My investigations have lead to a fish plant here in Emden. It could be that they will arrive in a barrel of fish and that the man who put them in there will try to get them back here. And that's when I want to step in.»

«You said, ‹the man›», Fiona remarked, «why do you think there's only one?»

«Do you think there's more than one?» Mary asked quickly.

«Well», Fiona explained, «we've seen two and –», hier versuchte Edzard, sie unterm Tisch mit einem Tritt vors Schienbein am Weiterreden zu hindern, traf aber nicht – «we think there is at least one other person involved.»

Mary Murphy reagierte sofort: «And what do they …» Edzard unterbrach sie noch einmal. «Warum sollte ein Mann allein so einen komischen unsicheren Schmuggelweg nehmen? Das ist doch eigentlich hirnrissig.»

Fiona translated what he had said even though she didn't really know what *hirnrissig* meant. «Yes», was the answer, «you're probably right. My contacts in the underworld said they heard that there were two of them, and that one wanted to double-cross the other. They claim that there was some kind of chase and that he had to get rid of the jewels somehow or other. But as I say, that's just a rumour. I know about one man for definite, and I know that he is here in Emden at the moment. Can you tell me what your men look like?»

Fiona didn't have to think long about it. «One of them is blond and he drives a green Golf. We think he may be Irish.»

«Yes, that's Freddy», said the woman, «he's the one I'm after.»

Fiona grinned at Edzard. «We were right!» Edzard freute sich aber kaum darüber. Er wünschte nur, dass Fiona aufhörte zu erzählen.

«And the other two?» Mary continued her questioning. Die lässt nicht locker, dachte Edzard. Na ja, wenn sie wirklich Detektivin ist, muss sie das alles natürlich brennend interessieren. «Well», said Fiona, «one of them has black hair, we think he's Irish too. He's always very elegantly dressed.» Ging da nicht für einen Moment ein Schreck durch Marys Gesicht? Edzard war sich nicht sicher. Ruhig sagte sie: «I don't know him at all. Are you sure he isn't just a tourist?» she asked.

«Like you?», warf Edzard ein. Mary tat so, als ob sie das nicht gehört hätte.

«And the third fellow?» she asked Fiona. «We haven't seen him yet», Fiona told her. «Then how do you know that there is a third man involved?»

«The black-haired fellow keeps phoning someone all the time, so we thought ...»

«You thought ...?» prompted Mary.

«We thought there must be a third person somewhere, too», übernahm Edzard, «but we think it's only a game really, nicht, Fiona? It's fun playing detectives during the holidays.» Er wollte vom Thema ablenken und Fiona zu verstehen geben, dass sie schon mehr als genug geredet hatte. Aber Mary ließ sich so schnell nicht abschütteln.

«And do you detectives have any idea when the jewels might arrive?» she continued.

«Yes, now, this minute! Come on, Fiona, we've got to catch the thief!» Edzard sprang von seinem Stuhl auf und zog Fiona am Arm. «Edzard, for goodness sake!» she pleaded. «Nun komm schon, we can't let the thief escape», drängelte er.

«Fiona», sagte Mary Murphy bedeutungsvoll, «just remember, if you do find out anything – you can trust me. I'd be grateful for your help.»

Fiona stieß Edzard von sich weg. «All right», she said to him, «stop acting the imbecile, I'm coming.» She turned to Mary:

«Sorry about this», she apologized, «maybe we'll bump into each other again another time. Bye!»

Schlagabtausch

«Wie kann man bloß so blöd sein!» und «You're so bloody paranoid!» waren noch die harmlosesten Sachen, die Edzard und Fiona sich in der nächsten Viertelstunde an den Kopf warfen. Für Edzard war die Frau eine neugierige Touristin oder, schlimmer noch, sie gehörte vielleicht zu den Dieben.

As far as Fiona was concerned, everything was clear now. No wonder Mary Murphy had been interested in Matjes, that she had been looking towards *Friesland Fisch* from the *Rathausturm*, and that she had been so curious all the time. As a detective working on the case, she had to be.

«Wie kann jemand ein scharfsinniger Detektiv sein, wenn er nicht mal Edzard und Edward auseinander halten kann?», schimpfte Edzard schließlich, nachdem ihm Fiona seine ganzen Argumente zerpflückt hatte.

Even though she was furious, Fiona had to smile. «Why don't you admit it; it's just because she's a woman that you don't believe she's a detective. If it was a John Murphy, tall and broadshouldered, wearing a trench-coat and a Humphrey Bogart hat, you'd be all on to cooperate with him and would gladly hand over the evidence, isn't that true?» Fiona said, half-jokingly.

«Es gibt keine richtigen Beweise», trotzte Edzard.

Fiona sighed. She wanted to go to the police straight away, or at least to tell Mary Murphy everything they knew.

«Die Polizei lacht uns nur aus», wehrte Edzard ab. «Und Mary Murphy? Na gut, wenn sie eine Detektivin ist, dann erklärt das ihr Verhalten», da gab er Fiona Recht, «trotzdem, ich traue ihr nun mal nicht.»

«Typical», said Fiona sarcastically, «why are we girls always the intelligent ones and you fellows only go by your feelings?» They could have spent the rest of the day arguing about it, but finally they reached an agreement. They would wait and see what happened that night. «And whatever we find out», added Fiona, «we'll either tell the police or else Mary Murphy.»

«Es sei denn, wir erwischen sie, wie sie im Fisch rumwühlt», stichelte Edzard.

«Oh shut up, Mr. Know-all», Fiona barked, and gave him a dirty look. After a while she asked: «Where are we going to Position ourselves this evening-up on the *Rathausturm*?»

«Die machen zu früh dicht», antwortete Edzard. «Einer muss wohl ins Versteck. Von da aus kann man beobachten, was alles über die Brücke kommt.»

«And where will the other one go?»

«Keine Ahnung. Ein zweites gutes Versteck gibt es nicht. Außer in 'nem Boot.»

Fiona laughed: «I assume the *Wassergeist* is occupied already.»

«Wir können natürlich beide ins Versteck gehen», überlegte Edzard, «aber dann ist ein Zugang unbeobachtet. Oder einer von uns fährt ab und zu mit dem Fahrrad an der Fabrik vorbei.»

Fiona didn't agree with that. «They know who we are now. It would be too obvious.»

«Dann muss sich einer ein bisschen weiter unten am Wasser postieren. Irgendwie unauffällig.»

«Hey!» Fiona had an idea. «You could pretend you're fishing there!»

«Nicht schlecht», stimmte Edzard zu, «dann geh ich jetzt nach Hause und besorg mein Angelzeug. Und vielleicht ein bisschen Proviant.»

«No fish for me, please.»

Sie verabredeten sich vorsichtshalber schon für halb sechs am Delft, obwohl vor Arbeitsschluss um sechs sicher nichts passieren würde. Edzard kam ziemlich beladen an. Außer Angelzeug und Fernglas, belegten Broten, Cola-Dosen und ein paar Äpfeln hatte er auch noch zwei Walkie-Talkies dabei.

«My God, where did you find them?» Fiona asked, pointing to the walkie-talkies.

«Hab ich mal zu Weihnachten bekommen. Damals bin ich zwei Tage damit um den Block gelaufen, und dann habe ich nie wieder was mit den Dingern gemacht. Aber heute Abend, wer weiß ...»

Fiona took one of the walkie-talkies. Neither of them said anything for a moment. «Well», Fiona broke the silence, «it's not really a game anymore now, is it?»

Edzard war auch etwas mulmig zumute. «Tja, jetzt sieht's ernst aus. Dann gehen wir mal auf unsere Posten, was?» They looked at each other. «Mensch, pass bloß auf», sagte er. «Mensch, you be bloß careful as well», she answered, and gave him a quick hug.

When Fiona arrived at the hide-out, she wondered what the hell she had let herself in for. What could they find out, anyway? The idea that they would be able to do anything to stop Freddy, the black-haired fellow, or even the mysterious Mr. X, was highly unlikely.

Hoffentlich fange ich keinen Fisch, dachte Edzard, als er die Angel auswarf. Er hatte sich so postiert, dass er den *Wassergeist* und die Zufahrtswege zu *Friesland Fisch* im Auge behielt.

I never would have thought that chasing people could be so boring, thought Fiona two hours later. Nothing had happened since she had left Edzard. Sitting around in this smelly hole wasn't really the most pleasant of all things to do. At first, she had tried to chat to Edzard on the walkie-talkie, but the sound was so distorted that they had given up after a while. Now their communication was reduced to: «Still nothing new» and «Hier auch nicht». The only bit of news so far from Edzard was that the green Golf AUR-B-815, the one which she had seen parked in front of the building after the interview with Herr Janssen for her project, had left *Friesland Fisch* shortly after six, with three people in it. Employees, obviously. ˉ

Es begann, dunkel zu werden. Über drei Stunden spielte Edzard jetzt schon erfolglos den Anglerspion. Gerade noch konnte er den *Wassergeist* erkennen.

«Edzard, can you hear me?», knatterte es aus dem Walkie-Talkie.

«Ja», Edzard merkte, wie sich alles in ihm anspannte, «was ist?»

«Nothing really. How much longer are we going to hang around here?»

«Keine Ahnung», gab Edzard zurück, «Mensch, ich dachte schon, bei dir ist endlich … du, Moment mal, der Schwarzhaarige klettert gerade an Deck!»

«What are you going to do now? Do you want to follow him?»

«Keine Ahnung …» Edzard unterbrach sich und steckte das Gerät weg. Auf der Straße rollte langsam ein Wagen ohne Licht an ihm vorbei, ein grüner Golf: AUR-B-375. Edzard wartete noch einen Moment, dann nahm er wieder Kontakt auf: «Fiona, hörst du mich?» Keine Antwort. «Fiona?»

«Yes, Edzard», knatterte es, «I'm on the bridge. I'm on my way over.»

«Pass gut auf», flüsterte Edzard. Hoffentlich ist sie vorsichtig, dachte er, legte die Angel beiseite, steckte das Sprechgerät in die Tasche und ging in Richtung *Friesland Fisch.*

Fiona crossed over the bridge. She thought she might position herself behind the stack of pallets again – the place where she and Edzard had hidden when the second break-in took place. If she approached it from the road, she'd be too close to the building, so she decided to move towards it from behind instead. She walked alongside the railway tracks and felt quite safe there: if a train came along, she knew she would hear the barriers of the level-crossing closing first. It was getting dark quickly now, she couldn't see much any more. When she got close to *Friesland Fisch,* she saw that someone else was just hiding behind the stack of pallets. She dropped down to the ground, lying close to the tracks. Thank God I didn't go straight there, she said to herself.

Der grüne Golf war in einiger Entfernung der Fischfabrik geparkt. Edzard blieb stehen. Er meinte erkennen zu können, dass der Blonde noch im Wagen saß und rauchte. Edzard wartete.

It was the black-haired fellow who was hiding behind the pallets, Fiona finally made out. Why was he waiting there, keeping watch on *Friesland Fisch*? Why didn't he go in, she wondered. Could it be that he was waiting for Freddy? Or even for Mr. X?

Die Wagentür ging auf, der Blonde stieg aus. Sich vorsichtig umschauend, näherte er sich dem Gebäude. Edzard schlich langsam weiter bis zum Wagen. Der gab ihm Deckung. Ob er Fiona etwas durchs Sprechgerät zuflüstern konnte? Lieber nicht, es war absolut still.

The black-haired fellow must have seen something. In the dark, Fiona thought she could make out how he tensed his muscles, ready for action. She could vaguely see someone moving towards the *Friesland Fisch* building. It was probably Freddy. She wondered whether she should try to say something to Edzard on the walkie-talkie, but she decided it would be too risky. The place was totally silent.

Der Blonde griff durch das zerschnittene Fliegengitter, öffnete das Fenster und stieg ein. Der hat ja schon Routine, dachte Edzard.

For quite a while nothing happened. The blond fellow was inside the plant, the black-haired fellow was keeping watch on it, and Fiona was keeping an eye on him. Then she heard the plink-

plink sound. The barriers of the level-crossing were going down. Shit, Fiona thought, I've got to move away from here fast. She looked around. Just then, the blond fellow climbed out the window, holding a small parcel in his hand. In no time at all, the black-haired man jumped up from behind the pallets and went for him. Fiona was relieved. Now she could go and take his place.

Mit ein paar Riesensätzen kam jemand hinter den aufgestapelten Paletten hervor. Es war der Schwarzhaarige. Er sprang auf den Blonden zu, packte mit beiden Händen an dessen Hals, würgte ihn und riss ihn zu Boden. Freddy schien diesmal jedoch weniger überrascht zu sein. Er warf das Päckchen zur Seite und wehrte sich.

The parcel landed only a few feet away from where Fiona was hiding. For the moment at least, the two men were occupied with beating each other up. Suddenly, the silence was broken by a shrill hoot. The train raced by, bright carriage after carriage rattling along through the darkness. They wouldn't hear her now if … Fiona was all excited. Should she risk it?

Edzard hielt den Atem an. Während der Eilzug von Hannover über die Brücke ratterte und die Stille der Nacht zerschnitt, huschte eine zweite Gestalt hinter den aufgestapelten Paletten hervor. Na endlich, der geheimnisvolle Mr. X, freute sich Edzard, der hatte sich da mit dem Schwarzhaarigen versteckt. Er sah genauer hin. Nicht möglich. Edzard biss sich in die Hand vor Aufregung. Das war nicht Mr. X, das war Fiona, die das Päckchen aufhob, ganz eindeutig. Bist du wahnsinnig, Fiona! Im letzten Moment bremste er sich noch, fast hätte er laut geschrien. Los, Fiona, lauf weg, lauf! Die beiden Männer schlugen immer noch aufeinander ein. Hoffentlich merken die nichts, betete Edzard.

Fiona ran and ran and ran. Her heart was pounding. She didn't stop before she reached the other side of the bridge. She looked back. No one was following her. She waited till she had got enough breath to speak, and then took out the walkie-talkie.

«Edzard!», hörte Edzard sie über das Sprechgerät keuchen, «Edzard, can you hear me? I've got it!» Edzard hatte sich sofort, als er gesehen hatte, dass Fiona weggelaufen war und dass die beiden immer noch miteinander kämpften, zurückgezogen. «Mensch, unglaublich! Einsame Klasse!», antwortete er. «I'm on my way to the ice-cream parlour now», Fiona said, «see you there.»

Sie trafen fast gleichzeitig dort ein und fielen sich in die Arme. «Wahnsinn!», japste Edzard. «Totaler Wahnsinn. Und was jetzt?»

«We'll open it up, look at it, and then it's off to the police station», Fiona declared, still puffing and panting.

«Aber nicht hier mitten auf der Hauptstraße.» Sie gingen in eine unbeleuchtete Nebenstraße.

The parcel consisted of a small padded envelope, wrapped up in a sealed plastic bag. Fionas hands were shaking as she opened it. Inside the envelope was a box.

So sehen Kästchen aus, die man bei einem Juwelier bekommt, um Schmuck darin aufzubewahren. Edzard war sich sicher, dass es mit Samt gefüttert war. They each held their breath as Fiona slowly opened the box. It was empty! Empty, that is, apart from a piece of paper with a message on it:

YOU DON'T ALWAYS MAKE a catch every time you go FISHing HArD LUCK !

Ratlos

They looked at each other in amazement. «Und jetzt?»

«Haven't a clue.» Damit hatten sie nun wirklich nicht gerechnet. Wer zum Teufel konnte das getan haben? «Bist du sicher, dass dich keiner von den beiden erkannt hat?», fragte Edzard besorgt.

«No, why?» Fiona asked back.

«Na, stell dir vor, du kloppst dich mit jemandem um ein Päckchen Diamanten, hinter denen du seit Ewigkeiten her bist, und da taucht eine andere Person auf und schnappt dir die Beute weg – wie würdest du reagieren?»

«But I didn't get the diamonds. They were gone already!»

«Das wissen die doch nicht.»

Fiona thought for a moment. «Hmm, well, in that case I think I would team up with the other fellow and then – oh God, Edzard – then I'd chase whoever it was who took the parcel. Does that mean that they'll be after me?»

«After us», verbesserte Edzard, «ich häng da genauso drin wie du.» They decided that there wasn't any point in going to the police then because they had absolutely nothing to show them that would prove their case.

«Tja», bestimmte Edzard schließlich, «dann werden wir uns wohl etwas länger mit Mary Murphy unterhalten müssen. Vielleicht weiß sie einen Ausweg.» Any other time or place Fiona would have had to smile at the idea of Edzard proposing that, but at the moment she was just too worried to find anything amusing.

Edzard verbrachte eine unruhige Nacht allein zu Haus. Alle Geräusche schienen so ungewohnt; hatten Freddy und der Schwarzhaarige schon herausgefunden, wo er wohnte, und versuchten einzubrechen? Edzard überlegte sich Fluchtwege aus dem Fenster, schob den Tisch vor die Wohnungstür und stellte Schüsseln so auf den Tisch, dass sie beim leichtesten Anstoß runterfallen konnten – es half aber alles nichts, er blieb halb wach, sprungbereit.

Je mehr Edzard über die ganze Sache nachdachte, desto klarer schien es ihm, dass eigentlich nur Mr. O'Donnell oder sogar Herr Janssen als Täter infrage kamen. Die Container waren angekommen und entladen worden, der Schwarzhaarige hatte offensichtlich die ganze Zeit auf dem Boot verbracht, und Freddy war erst kurz vor dem Kampf mit seinem Golf angerollt gekommen – beide konnten die Juwelen also nicht vorher vertauscht haben. Nur Mr. O'Donnell, Herr Janssen und dessen Angestellte hatten vorher die Möglichkeit gehabt, an die Fässer heranzukommen. Oder hätte Freddy in der kurzen Zeit, in der er im Lager war, die Juwelen nehmen und einfach ein zweites Päckchen heraustragen können? Aber dann hätte er gewusst haben müssen, dass draußen …

Edzard wälzte sich im Bett hin und her. Das war viel zu konstruiert. Nein, alles sprach eigentlich gegen Mr. O'Donnell. Und Mary Murphy war überhaupt nicht in Erscheinung getreten. Er hatte sie wohl wirklich zu Unrecht verdächtigt. Na ja, rechtfertigte er sich, Vorsicht ist besser als Nachsicht, jetzt wusste er wenigstens, dass man ihr trauen konnte.

Mr. Burke thought he was seeing things when he got up for work and found his daughter in the kitchen. «You're up very early today, Fiona», he remarked, «anything the matter?» Now would be the time to tell him, Fiona thought to herself but she wanted to talk it all over with Edzard again first.

«What? Oh no, nothing wrong. It's a kind of a race to see who gets to the Delft first this morning, that's all», she lied.

«A competition? I see. And who's the other early bird you're racing against? Hilke?» Fiona smiled. Hilke would still be enjoying her beauty sleep at that hour of the morning. «No, he's a rather good-looking blond actually.» She thought she'd give her father that much information. «A good-looking fellow at this hour of the morning! Very strange. In my day we always tried to arrange to get together as late as possible in the evening. Well, times are changing, I suppose.» Fiona wanted to get away quickly. «I'll let you know who wins, Dad, I've got to run now», she said, grabbed a slice of toast and raced off.

Frau Heerma traute ihren Augen nicht, als Edzard im Treppenhaus an ihr vorbeistürmte. «Was denn, schon auf?», fragte sie, aber da war Edzard schon an ihr vorbeigerauscht.

Die Eisdiele hatte natürlich noch zu, als beide ankamen. «Wir müssen heute wohl ein bisschen länger auf unsere tägliche Dosis warten», versuchte Edzard zu scherzen, aber zum Lachen war ihnen nicht zumute.

«I've been thinking, Edzard», Fiona began.

«Schau mal einer an», unterbrach er sie, «sie hat nachgedacht. Meinst du, ich hätte die ganze Nacht sanft geschlummert, ohne mir das alles tausendmal durch den Kopf gehen zu lassen?»

Fiona was amazed. He wasn't normally that touchy. He mustn't have slept at all the night before. «O. k., calm down. There's no point in us arguing. We only have each other to depend on now.» She sounded upset.

«'tschuldigung, Fiona, ich wollte dich nicht angreifen. Ich hab bloß die ganze Nacht wach gelegen und eine Lösung gesucht. Wir sind da ganz schön in etwas hineingeraten.»

Fiona tried to cheer him up: «You'd never know, Edzard, maybe Freddy and the black-haired fellow murdered each other last night and then the whole problem is solved.»

«Oder noch besser: Die beiden haben sich gegenseitig k. o. geschlagen, sind dabei ins Wasser gefallen, Mr. O'Donnell ist ihnen hinterhergesprungen, und Herr Janssen und Mary Murphy sind wiederum ihm nach. Dabei sind leider alle ums Leben gekommen, und kein Schwein weiß mehr was von den Diamanten – außer uns beiden. Und Dolly natürlich.» Edzard ging es schon wieder ein bisschen besser. Zu zweit und bei Tage sah alles weniger schlimm aus als nachts allein zu Haus.

«Sorry to disappoint you, Edzard», Fiona said suddenly, «but one of your candidates must have made it out of the water. Here comes Mary Murphy. But we know now that she's on our side, so it's o. k.»

Mary Murphy stopped when she reached the ice-cream parlour. «It's not a bad thing knowing where to find you two, but isn't it a bit early in the day for ice-cream?» she said loud and cheerfully. Then she looked around and lowered her voice: «Have you got them with you?»

Edzard and Fiona waren verblüfft. «What?» Fiona managed to say. «The jewels», Mary replied, «you managed to get away with them yesterday evening. Good work. Congratulations.»

«Woher wissen … ich meine … how do you know?», stotterte Edzard. Mary laughed. «I wasn't hiding as obviously as you, Mr. Fisherman, but I was there all the same. I saw what happened but decided it was better to let the two of you disappear alone. If the men had noticed anything I could have diverted their attention. And anyway, jewels don't go rotten overnight, so I could wait till today. Have you got them with you now?»

Fiona und Edzard schauten sich einen Moment an. «There were no jewels in the parcel, Mary», Fiona said. Das Lächeln verschwand aus Marys Gesicht. «What do you mean?»

«I mean someone else got there before us», Fiona explained. Mary überlegte einen Moment und sagte dann scharf: «Look, clever little missy, my company is offering a reward to the person who finds the stolen jewels. You needn't worry that you won't get anything out of all this, but it wouldn't be very clever if you were to try to go it alone and sell them somewhere. Then there's bound to be trouble.»

Na ja, ich würde uns an ihrer Stelle auch nicht glauben, dachte Edzard, holte den anonymen Brief aus seiner Tasche und zeigte ihn ihr. Sie sah ihn ungläubig an: «And this was all that was in the parcel?» she asked. Beide nickten. «Who could have got there first?» Mary wondered.

«Mr. O'Donnell», antworteten beide gleichzeitig. «Er ist Mr. X und hat die beiden anderen ausgetrickst», erklärte Edzard. Mary looked to Fiona for help. «What did he say and who is this Mr. O'Donnell fellow?» she asked. Fiona sighed. «That's a long story. Let's go somewhere and sit down and we'll tell you all about it.»

Eine halbe Stunde später wusste Mary Murphy genau, was Edzard und Fiona im Verlauf der letzten Woche alles erlebt hatten. «He could have got at the barrels before the others, and it would also explain why he was acting so suspiciously», Fiona concluded.

«So it looks like your Mr. X managed to double-cross his partners as well, then», Mary added with a grin, «quite a clever chap, isn't he?» Edzard fand das gar nicht lustig. «Freddy und der Schwarzhaarige haben sich inzwischen bestimmt zusammengetan und sind jetzt hinter uns her», sagte er.

After Fiona had translated that, Mary Murphy looked a bit worried. «You could be right. It seems the logical thing for them to do. If I were you I'd keep a low profile for a while. Maybe you should leave Emden until things get sorted out», she suggested.

«We could always go to the police and tell them our story. If you came along they might believe us», Fiona said. «No, I don't think they would», answered Mary, «we don't have any proof and anyway, if they start asking questions and arresting people I'll never get the jewels. If you two disappear for a while, I'll try to get a lead on this Mr. O'Donnell person and the jewels, and then we can go to the police together. What about that?»

Edzard und Fiona waren unsicher. Mary tried again: «Well, let's say I'll try to find out as much as I can today and we'll meet … it's half eight now … let's say we'll meet at the ice-cream parlour at half four, and regardless of what I have or haven't found out by then we'll go to the police.»

Dem konnten Edzard und Fiona schon leichter zustimmen. «Na toll, wir hauen gleich ab. Ich kann dir dann endlich mal ein bisschen Ostfriesland zeigen. Wir fahren an den Deich, oder ich zeig dir die Fischerboote in Greetsiel oder so», schlug Edzard Fiona vor und sagte dann zu Mary Murphy: «We'll do some sightseeing away from Emden and will come back to meet you at half past four.»

«Good idea», replied Mary, «maybe you should take this with you. It's the address of the hotel I'm staying at. Just in case something happens and you're back later or earlier or whatever.» She turned to Fiona. «I was up a lovely tower yesterday in a place called Mariahafen or something like that. There's a great story about a pirate attached to it.»

«Ja, der Störtebekerturm in Marienhafe», unterbrach Edzard, «von da aus hast du 'ne tolle Aussicht, und das schaffen wir auch bis half fünf.»

«A pirate!» Fiona laughed. «How appropriate. Nothing to do with fish though, I hope.» They waved good-bye to Mary and cycled off.

Kidnapped

Bright sunshine and a gentle breeze. Fiona loved cycling in that kind of weather, and flying past the green meadows with their black and white cows would normally have put her into a fantastic mood. But she just couldn't relax and enjoy it. Not after all that had happened in the past two days. She tried to take her mind off things. «Who is that pirate fellow anyway?» she asked Edzard.

«Störtebeker? Man sagt – ob das alles stimmt, weiß ich nicht –, also es heißt, dass er von Marienhafe aus mit seinen Männern Schiffe gekapert ... gekapert, äh, überfallen hat, meistens Schiffe der Hanse ... Hanse, Gott, das ist schwer zu erklären, das ist ein Zusammenschluss von Städten gewesen, deren Kaufleute Handel zur See betrieben und ...» Edzard merkte, dass er sich mit seiner Erklärung verhedderte. «Ist ja auch egal, der ist bei uns so was wie bei euch Robin Hood: he robbed the rich to help the poor. Marienhafe war der Stützpunkt von Störtebekers Bande, dort haben sie ihre Beute verteilt. Und der Turm der Kirche half ihnen bei der Navigation.»

Climbing the church tower in Marienhafe was quite an exciting affair. Under normal circumstances they would probably have imagined all kinds of spooky stories and adventures on their way up, but now they felt there was enough happening in reality without having to invent things as well. Fiona was surprised at how flat the surrounding landscape was when she looked down. She saw a few windmills from the top of the tower, and a church sticking out in the distance, but she couldn't see the sea. That was strange. How could that Störtebeker fellow have used the church tower as a point of navigation if it was so far inland? Maybe she could see it from one of the other three sides of the tower.

She just wanted to ask Edzard about the missing sea when she looked down and saw a green Golf parked on the street below. Come on, Fiona, she said to herself after her heart had jumped, there are hundreds of green Golfs in Germany. They are made here, after all. Relax, for God's sake. As they were turning around the corner she asked Edzard: «Can we see the sea from the other …» A heavy steel band closed around her heart and made the last word stick in her throat. Standing directly in front of them, with a nasty grin on his face, was the black-haired fellow.

Einen Augenblick lang schienen beide zu erstarren. Dann aber liefen sie los. So schnell wie möglich jagten sie mit gebeugten Köpfen den engen, in Stein gehauenen Wendelgang hinunter. Kurz vor der Zwischenebene liefen sie auf eine Touristengruppe auf, Vater, Mutter, Oma, Kleinkind. Das Kind quengelte, die Oma beschwerte sich über die ausgelatschten Stufen. God! Why couldn't they move more quickly. It was too narrow to pass them by on the steps. Fortunately they just reached a kind of floor in between where the bells and lots of other interesting things to look at were. Fiona und Edzard konnten keinen Gedanken auf all die Holzstreben, Räderwerke für die Glocken und die gruselige Atmosphäre dieses Rondells verwenden, sie freuten sich nur, dass sie an der Gruppe vorbeijagen konnten, zur nächsten Wendeltreppe, weniger eng diesmal, aber länger.

Fiona felt very dizzy racing down the spiral stairs, but she knew they had to keep going. They rushed past the exhibition in the room at the bottom of the stairs, flew out the door and down the steps that led into the graveyard below, ran to the gate where their bicycles were – they knew the black-haired fellow was getting closer – reached the gate, got to their bicycles and were suddenly grabbed from behind by two strong arms which threw them onto the back seat of a parked car. The green Golf. Freddy got in beside them and held the point of a knife between Fiona's ribs.

«One word from either of you and she gets it», he threatened, «just keep smiling, like good kids, while we take you for a little ride.» The black-haired fellow was down there now, he got into the driver's seat, started up the car, and off they drove.

Während der Fahrt blieben die beiden Männer stumm; Freddy saß mit seinem Messer so nahe bei Fiona, dass an eine Flucht bei einer roten Ampel nicht zu denken war. Die Männer brachten sie zum *Wassergeist* und stießen sie unter Deck. Freddy zündete sich eine Zigarette an, blies Fiona den Rauch ins Gesicht und sagte: «Well, madam, would you mind telling us where the diamonds are?»

Fiona sah Edzard an, Edzard sah Fiona an. Was sollte man ihnen erzählen? Die Wahrheit? Die glaubten sie ja doch nicht. Aber sie konnten sich ja schließlich keine Diamanten herzaubern.

«You won't believe me, but …» Fiona began. «Then you'd better tell us something we can believe, hadn't you?» the black-haired fellow interrupted. «Our Freddy there is a very nervous type of man. He might just let his cigarette fall onto your face if he didn't believe what you were saying.»

Fiona looked anxiously at Freddy and his cigarette. «But it's true and we can prove it. There were no jewels in the parcel, just a letter», she blurted out. «Just a letter! That's a good one!» said Freddy as he and his cigarette moved closer to Fiona's face. «It's true!» Edzard shouted. «Here, look at it.» Er zeigte ihnen den anonymen Brief.

«Not bad at all, you're very clever for your age», said the black-haired man in a friendly tone after he had read the letter, then all of a sudden he slapped Edzard across the face and screamed: «Do you think you can fool us, you stupid brats? As if you didn't have enough time to do this yourselves. But I'm warning you, we want the jewels and we want them now.»

«I have an idea, Luke», Freddy said, «I'll take the girl and we'll go and pick up the stuff wherever they've hidden it. She has two hours to tell me where it is, and if she doesn't, well, then it's *his* bad luck.»

Er deutete auf Edzard und machte eine eindeutige Bewegung mit dem Zeigefinger am Hals. Dann schneiden wir ihm die Kehle durch, hieß das. Edzard fühlte, wie ihm der Schweiß aus allen Poren rann. «But it's true», stotterte er, «we don't have them, Mr. O'Donnell does.»

Die beiden schien diese Erklärung nicht besonders zu beeindrucken. Außerdem stieß Freddys Vorschlag bei seinem Partner nicht auf Zustimmung. «You and the girl, Freddy, I see. But I don't think it's a good idea. I wouldn't put it past you to get up to your double-crossing tricks again. I think we should let her go on her own and get the jewels from wherever they are hiding them, or from Mr. O'Donnell whoever he is. And if she doesn't deliver the goods …» Er wiederholte Freddys Geste. Dann fiel ihm was Besseres ein. «Or maybe we should send *him* instead», fuhr er fort, «fellows always like to protect pretty young girls, don't they? We'll keep her here as a security.»

Fiona felt sick. «You're a suspicious bastard, but o. k.», Freddy agreed, «we'll send the boy on his own then.» He turned to Edzard, blew smoke into his eyes and said: «But remember, if you're not back here with the jewels in two hours time – and without doing anything stupid like getting in touch with the police – you won't be able to recognize your girl's pretty face ever again.»

Die Falle

Außer Sichtweite des Bootes musste Edzard erst mal kotzen. Er wusste nicht, was er machen sollte. Die Juwelen hatte er nicht, und zur Polizei gehen wollte er eigentlich auch nicht, um Fiona nicht zu gefährden. Alles mit Mary Murphy zu bereden erschien ihm noch am wenigsten unsinnig. Obwohl sie die Juwelen natürlich auch nicht herbeizaubern konnte. Es war lange vor der verabredeten Zeit, aber er hoffte, dass er sie in ihrem Hotel antreffen würde.

Er hatte Glück, Mary war da. So schnell und so ausführlich, wie es sein Englisch ihm erlaubte, berichtete er ihr, was seit dem Morgen passiert war. Mary hörte zu, unterbrach nur ab und zu mit ein paar Nachfragen.

«And what have you found out about Mr. O'Donnell?», fragte Edzard am Ende. «Nothing much, really, we don't have a file on him», antwortete Mary, «but forget about him for the moment. The important question now is how to get Fiona out of the boat safely.» Sie überlegte einen Moment. «We don't have the jewels so we can't give them to the men. And even if we had them …» Sie führte den Satz nicht zu Ende.

Edzard starrte sie an:

«If we did we would hand them over to save Fiona's life», sagte er entschlossen. Mary nickte nachdenklich. «I suppose you're right.» Edzard fuhr fort: «Dann müssen wir, äh, then we have to go to the police, and we have to go there quickly. Wer weiß, I mean, who knows what will happen to Fiona otherwise?»

Mary Murphy zögerte. «Yes», she said finally, «we'll have to go to the police all right. But we can't afford to waste any more time.» Sie sah auf ihre Uhr. «You've only got about an hour left. And a boat in the water is probably one of the worst possible places for a police raid.»

Sie zündete sich eine Zigarette an. «Smoke?» Sie bot Edzard eine an. «No thanks. But we have to do something.» Er war verzweifelt.

«Wait now, wait now!» Mary schien plötzlich ganz aufgeregt zu sein. «Maybe that would work.» Edzard schöpfte Hoffnung. «Look», sagte Mary, «you could go back to the boat and say something like this: Of course I have the jewels, but I didn't bring them with me – I'm not a total idiot. I didn't bring them back here because there's no guarantee that you would let Fiona and me go safely if I did. You could get rid of us and nobody would know. I've hidden the jewels somewhere where we can go to in the boat now. It's a public place where we can be seen, and Fiona and I and one of you can leave the boat to get the jewels. You can take them and we can go.»

Das geht bestimmt nicht gut, dachte Edzard, und außerdem, was passiert dann? Ich hab die Dinger schließlich nicht. Mary fuhr fort: «And while you are telling them all this, I will have gone to the police and will convince them to go to the place and wait for the men, wherever it is you tell them to go. Do you understand what I'm telling you?» Edzard nickte. Das war immerhin ein Plan.

«Can you think of a place, which can be reached by boat and where the police could remain hidden until the two of you and one of the men are on land? They'd have to be able to get at the fellow in the boat from there, too», Mary added, «and it shouldn't be too near where the boat is now. The longer it takes you to get there, the more time the police have to get themselves organized.»

Einen Moment lang war es völlig leer in Edzards Gehirn. Dann fiel ihm die Kleine Seeschleuse ein. Dort musste man vom Boot aus erst mal ein Stück zur Straße laufen. Die Polizei könnte die beiden dann getrennt angreifen. Mary fand den Vorschlag gut. «I'll drive to the police station straight away», sagte sie, «and you should start making your way back to the boat. I hope you're a good actor.» Sie legte ihren Arm um seine Schultern. «Don't worry, Edzard, we'll get Fiona back all right.» Eigentlich hätte ihn das trösten sollen, stattdessen jagte es ihm einen kalten Schauer über den Rücken.

«You're late! What took you so bloody long, you little bastard?», schrie Freddy, als Edzard zum Boot zurückkam. Er stieß ihn unsanft unter Deck, wo Fiona aufsprang und ihn umarmte.

«Gut, dass du o. k. bist», sagte Edzard erleichtert. Beide hatten Tränen in den Augen. «Ich …» – «Shut up talking German», Freddy roared, «where are the diamonds?»

«Not on me», antwortete Edzard tapfer und versuchte, Freddys Schlag auszuweichen. «Stop», rief er, «let me explain.»

Freddy, der Edzard inzwischen am Hals gepackt hatte, hielt einen Moment inne. Luke, der elegante Schwarzhaarige, kam unter Deck. «Not so loud, gentlemen», he said with a friendly smile and then gave the order in a cold voice: «Take the girl. I'd bet he wouldn't like to see his little star with stripes all over her face.»

Fiona was shaking. What the hell was Edzard playing at? Why had he come back? They didn't have a chance without the diamonds. She felt Freddy's cold, sharp knife on her skin and started to cry. «There, there, little girl, don't cry», said Luke sweetly, «I'm sure your shining knight here will come up with an explanation.» Er zündete sich eine Zigarette an und musterte Edzard mit stechendem Blick.

«Well, I ... äh, the diamonds ... äh», stotterte Edzard. «I've hidden them in a safe place. We can go there now in the boat. Then one of you and the two of us will get out, and we'll swop our freedom for the jewels», stieß er dann hervor. Er atmete tief durch. Jetzt war es raus. Was würde passieren?

Luke kam direkt auf ihn zu, starrte ihm in die Augen und bewegte seine Zigarette langsam auf Edzards Nasenwurzel zu. Fiona couldn't bear to look at it. What was he talking about? They hadn't got the jewels. Was it part of some plan? Anyway, no matter what it was, she should play along with it.

«Edzard!» she suddenly screamed. «Our jewels! What about the reward money we were going to get from the insurance company? All our plans. Trip around the world, luxury hotels, beaches, sunshine. You can't give our jewels to these bastards! I'm the one who got them and I'm not giving them away again.» Before Freddy could stop her, she jumped on top of Edzard and started to attack him.

Einen Sekundenbruchteil war Edzard verblüfft, dann begriff er. Klasse! Das würde die beiden Typen bestimmt überzeugen. Er hätte sie viel lieber umarmt als mit ihr gekämpft.

«But I had to», sagte er auf Englisch, «otherwise they would kill us.» Einen Moment sah es so aus, als verlören die beiden Gangster die Kontrolle über das Geschehen. Dann übernahm Luke wieder das Kommando. Er und Freddy zogen die beiden auseinander.

«O. k., o. k.», said Luke, «so the letter was a fake after all. Not bad, young man, not bad at all. Now, where are the jewels?»

Edzard erklärte seinen Plan.

«It's a trap», fluchte Freddy, als er die Einzelheiten hörte, «the brat has probably been to the police.» Er warf Edzard einen giftigen Blick zu. «It's not what we had arranged. I don't like it.»

«Maybe he has been to the police, maybe he hasn't», replied Luke, «but we haven't got much choice, have we? Either we beat the shit out of him and he still tells us the same story, or else he's telling the truth and then everything is just as he says it is. There's one change I'd like to make though», he said grinning at Freddy, «the two of us should get out of the boat with the two of them. We don't want to tempt anyone unnecessarily now, do we?»

«All right», brummelte Freddy, ging nach oben und machte die Leinen los.

Show-down

On their way towards the lock they had to pass through the two open bridges. As they were going through, Fiona remembered how she had crossed over the bridge and Edzard had crashed into her. It wasn't even a week ago! If only it had never happened. Now she felt she would have much preferred a boring holiday, only occasionally doing something with her father, to this. When she thought of her father she felt a lump in her throat and her eyes filled with tears. Would she ever see him again?

She still didn't know what Edzard's plan was. Had he gone to Mary Murphy or to the police – or to both? Who or what was waiting for them at the lock? That the jewels weren't there was clear to her. A special police squad, perhaps? She didn't fancy the idea of being held hostage with a knife at her back if the men saw that the police were there. And that's probably what it would boil down to. But maybe the police had thought of that already and had decided that they'd have a better chance of getting them when they were out of the boat at the lock than when they were inside it at the Delft.

Nach einigen Minuten bekamen sie nasse Füße. Wasser begann ins Vorderschiff zu laufen. «Bloody hell, what's that? Freddy!» Luke roared. Freddy came down. «My God», he said when he saw what was happening, «how do we get rid of it?» Edzard wurde blass. Eindringendes Wasser gehörte nicht zum Plan. Immerhin, mit Booten dieser Art kannte er sich aus.

«Der Schalter für die Lenzpumpe, äh, the switch for the ...», er suchte nach dem englischen Wort und sah Fiona fragend an. She shrugged her shoulders. «For the pump for the water is up there where you are steering. I think it's the third from the right», erklärte er Freddy. Der ging wieder nach oben.

Das Wasser lief weiter ein. Ganz schön schnell.

«Nothing is happening, the bloody pump doesn't work», Freddy shouted down after a few minutes. Das Wasser stieg. So schaffen wir das nie bis zur Seeschleuse, vorher sinken wir, durchfuhr es Edzard. Wir müssen an Land.

«Listen», sagte er zu Luke, «we can't go to the lock now, we have to save ourselves.»

«We'll make it to the lock all right», antwortete der ungerührt, «and after that we won't need this old tub any more anyway.»

Bis dahin kommen wir nie, dachte Edzard, wir müssen hier raus. Plan und Falle hin oder her, er entschloss sich zum Äußersten.

«There are no jewels at the lock. I lied», gestand er. Fiona held her breath. What would Luke do now? Throw them over board? Surprisingly enough he remained completely calm. « Yes there are », he replied, « you didn't lie. »

Edzard war außer sich. « It's a *Falle*, äh, the police are waiting for you there. Believe me! » Fiona felt her heart sink. Oh God, now they were really in for it. Aber Luke lachte nur.

« Did someone help you with your little plan? The insurance company detective Mary Murphy, maybe? She told you she would have the police waiting for us at the lock, didn't she? Not bad! »

Fiona couldn't believe her ears. How did he know Mary Murphy? She couldn't be ... Oh no! She looked at Edzard. He seemed to be staying remarkably cool. He just stared Luke straight in the eye.

« Oh yes », Luke continued. « Sarah Brady asked me to send you her love. That's Mary Murphy's real name, by the way. She said she found it very funny that you kept talking about a *Mr.* X all the time. It was a *Ms.* X after all. Gangster's lib, you know! » Er lachte wieder. « She and I came here on Freddy's heels. The three of us started out together. We did the Tiffen job as a three-some. Then the bastard double-crossed us. We chased after him, but somehow he managed to get rid of the jewels in Dunmore East. We kept on his trail which led us here, found out that he had hidden them in a barrel of fish, and waited to see what would happen. When they finally arrived and I tried to get them off him, well, that's when madam here stepped in », he nodded to Fiona, « and stole them off us. Sarah, or Mary as you call her, followed the two of you and saw that you didn't go to the police. You obviously wanted to keep the jewels for yourselves. She told you that you could get a nice fat reward from the insurance company if you handed the jewels over to her. She was full of admiration for you, I have to tell you that. Said you were very clever, not saying where the jewels were before you actually got the money. But you see, you were just that little bit too clever. She told you to go off for the day to that tower while she would organize your reward money. And you know the rest, don't you? Freddy just wanted to beat the information out of you about where you had hidden the jewels, but Sarah said she knew a better trick. We should let one of you go to her and she would tell you that it would be best for you to swop the jewels for your freedom. Well, you're obviously even smarter than she had thought, so she had to arrange this silly new plan with the hand-over in public. But that's o.k. with us. As long as we get the jewels back we're happy. So the police aren't at the lock but the jewels are, and so is Sarah with her car, I imagine.»

Edzard sah zu Fiona hinüber. Hoffentlich macht sie nicht schlapp, dachte er. Sie hockte inzwischen völlig apathisch auf dem Tisch und murmelte nur vor sich hin: «It's not true, it's just not true.» Er merkte, wie das Wasser weiter stieg.

«Half of your story is true», sagte Edzard möglichst gleich-gültig, «Mary Murphy wasn't a real insurance detective. I felt that all the time. That's o.k. But the second half is wrong. We don't have the jewels, and we never had them. *She* has them. I don't know how she did it, but she got there before you. The letter is real – she must have written it. And we are sinking. We have to reach the land.»

Er sah, wie Fiona ihn ungläubig anstarrte. Die Arme, dachte Edzard, für sie war bis eben Mr. O'Donnell Mr. X, dann hab ich erzählt, dass ich die Juwelen an der Schleuse versteckt hab, und nun behaupte ich auch noch, ich hätte schon gewusst, dass Mary Murphy Mr. X ist und dass sie die Juwelen hat.

Luke verlor die Beherrschung. «For Christ's sake, Freddy», he roared up the stairs, «will you get the pump going or else speed up. We have to get to the lock before the boat sinks.»

Drohend ging er auf Edzard zu. Er packte ihn am T-Shirt: «Look you, cut out the wise-cracks and shut up. We'll make it to the lock and Sarah and the jewels will be there. All according to plan. If not, you and your girl can start saying your prayers.»

Das Wasser stieg unaufhaltsam weiter. Lange würden sie nicht mehr auf dem Boot bleiben können. Wie konnte er sie nur über-zeugen?

«Look, Freddy double-crossed the two of you», versuchte Edzard es noch einmal, «and now she's double-crossing you and Freddy. I'm telling you, she has the jewels. Can't you see how stupid it is to go to the lock. I would never have hidden the jewels there. Do you really think I wouldn't have swopped the jewels for Fiona straight away? It's all that woman's plan. It's a trap. She said we should go somewhere in the boat, not me. She wants to drown us all. And if that doesn't work, she probably hopes the police will get you for kidnapping. Either way she'll be rid of you and can keep the jewels for herself.»

Luke schlug zu, seine Faust traf Edzards Magengrube. Edzard fiel ins Wasser. Fiona schrie auf, stürzte sich auf Luke, der warf sie zurück und wollte gerade wieder auf Edzard los, als Freddy herunterkam, mit einem Kabel in der Hand.

«Someone has sabotaged the pump. There's a bit missing», sagte er tonlos. Luke ließ von Edzard ab. «I don't believe it … She wouldn't have …would she? … The bitch!» schrie er. «The double-crossing bitch! Get the dinghy ready.»

They went up on deck. Freddy lowered the dinghy into the water. «Cheerio, young detectives», sagte Luke freundlich und stieß beide plötzlich mit aller Wucht ins Wasser. «Enjoy your swim», rief er ihnen nach, als er und Freddy im Beiboot losruderten.

When Fiona surfaced, she looked around for Edzard. «Are you o.k.?» She swam over to him. «Can you swim?» – «So lala, und du?» Fiona shook the wet hair out of her eyes. «Best in my class!» she said. «They've gone, Edzard, we're free, yippee! I could jump up and down only I'd probably sink. Anyway, we'd better save our energy. We've quite a bit to swim, and the wet clothes don't make it any easier. We should take off our shoes, though. They'll weigh us down.» They kicked off their shoes and let them sink to the bottom of Emden harbour. Zum Glück war das Wasser an diesem Tag ziemlich ruhig, aber auch so dauerte es mit den nassen Klamotten einige Zeit, bis sie sich aus dem Wasser ziehen konnten.

«Where are we?» Fiona asked after she had climbed out. «In Sicherheit», keuchte Edzard.

«We're safe, but apart from that things are pretty shitty, aren't they? They've got away, the jewels are gone, and Mary Murphy or Sarah whatever-she's-called is probably laughing herself silly about us.»

«Da wär ich nicht so sicher», lachte Edzard. «Oh come on», Fiona groaned, «don't tell me there's yet another version of the story. I'm confused enough as it is. Why don't you tell me what happened after you left the boat?»

Edzard erzählte von seiner Verzweiflung, von seinem Treffen mit Mary Murphy und von deren Plan. «Und als sie dann in ihren Wagen stieg und zur Polizei fuhr, da hatte ich plötzlich, na, wie soll ich das beschreiben, da gab's plötzlich 'ne Menge Bilder in meinem Kopf, so wie 'ne Rückblende im Film. Alles ging ineinander über. Sie sagt Matjes, das Fernglas in Richtung *Friesland Fisch* auf dem Rathausturm, dann, wie sie dich ausfragt …»

«But …», Fiona wanted to interrupt, aber Edzard war nicht zu bremsen. «Ich weiß, das hatten wir alles entkräftet. Aber trotzdem. Irgendwie hat *sie* uns doch geraten, nicht zur Polizei zu gehen. Und dann: Kannst du dich erinnern an das eine Telefongespräch? Da muss der Mr. X so was gesagt haben wie: Ich kümmere mich um die beiden. Und hat Mr. O'Donnell sich je ‹um uns gekümmert›? Nee, aber Mary Murphy tauchte dauernd auf. Als wir ihr zum ersten Mal erzählt hatten, was wir wussten, sagte sie, sie wäre auch hinter Freddy her, aber der Schwarzhaarige hätte nichts mit der Sache zu tun. Klar, dass sie den Verdacht von ihm ablenken wollte, wenn sie zusammen mit ihm hinter Freddy her war. Und dann fragte ich mich, war das nur Zufall, dass die beiden uns in Marienhafe gefangen haben? Wer wusste, dass wir gerade dahin fahren? Mary Murphy! Sie hat es uns sogar empfohlen.»

«Yes, but there are easier ways to kidnap people than to chase them from the top of a tower», Fiona interrupted.

«Tja, darüber hab ich mich auch gewundert. Das passte nicht. Aber jetzt ist es klar. Sie brauchte Zeit, um im Boot ein paar Dichtungen zu zerstören und die Pumpe außer Betrieb zu setzen. Ist auch egal, ich geb ja zu, das waren alles keine Beweise.

Ich hatte eben plötzlich so ein Gefühl. Ich bin in ein Taxi gesprungen und zur Polizei gefahren. Ich hatte Recht: Dort war keine Versicherungsdetektivin Mary Murphy angekommen. Es hat eine ganze Weile gedauert, bis ich jemand gefunden hatte, der mir meine Geschichte geglaubt hat.»

«No wonder it took you so long to get back to the boat then!» Fiona exclaimed. «The men were really on edge at that stage. Freddy kept saying: ‹I knew that plan wouldn't work.› I thought he just meant that letting you go away to get the jewels wouldn't work, but now I see that there was more to it than that. It was the plan Mary Murphy had fooled them into believing. What a wicked bitch! She really managed to trick everybody. Anyway, go on.»

«Die von der Polizei haben gesagt, dass man dich an der Seeschleuse tatsächlich viel besser befreien könnte als unten im Boot. Also haben sie erst mal schnell ein paar Leute in Marys Hotel geschickt. Und mit mir haben sie überlegt, wie's weitergehen soll. Das Beste war, ich sollte so tun, als ob Marys Plan geklappt hätte und zurück aufs Boot gehen. Dass sie den beiden Typen wieder einen anderen Plan erzählt hatte und dass sie die Bootsfahrt erfunden hatte, um den *Wassergeist* zum Kentern zu bringen, konnte ich ja nicht wissen. Deswegen wusste ich auf dem Boot auch nicht, ob ich den beiden gleich die ganze Wahrheit erzählen sollte, um sie zu bewegen, an Land zu fahren, oder ob ich erst mal so tun sollte, als liefe alles weiter nach Marys Plan. Du weißt ja nie, wie die reagieren, wenn sie mitkriegen, dass sie geleimt worden sind.»

«That was really good thinking, Edzard. And it would have worked out the way you planned if that cow hadn't wanted to drown us all», Fiona said, «but still, I suppose when we haven't arrived at the lock, the police will search the water for the four of us. They'll pick up Freddy and Luke anyway, if not on the water than they'll get them when they go to look for Mary in the hotel. But tell me this, does she really have the jewels or did you make up that part of the story?»

«Ich glaub, sie hat sie. Mit all diesen Tricks wollte sie nur erreichen, dass ihre Kumpane glauben, dass jemand anders die Juwelen hat. Wenn sie einfach mit den Dingern abgehauen wäre, dann hätten die beiden anderen sie so gejagt, wie sie und Luke Freddy gejagt haben. Und das wollte sie vermeiden. Wenn wir nicht dazwischengekommen wären, hätten sie den Brief gefunden, hätten verzweifelt überlegt, von wem der war, und hätten ohne Erfolg weitergesucht. Irgendwann hätten alle die Schnauze voll gehabt und aufgehört. Dann wäre noch ein bisschen Gras über die Sache gewachsen, und sie hätte schließlich allein das große Geld kassiert. Wahrscheinlich hat sie die Dinger schon in Dunmore East aus dem Fass herausgeholt und die Verfolgung von Freddy und den Juwelen bloß mitgespielt. Oder sie ist irgendwie vor den beiden in die Fabrik gekommen und hat dort die Juwelen gegen den Brief ausgetauscht.»

«So she wrote the letter to make Luke believe that there was another person involved who took them, that they hadn't just got lost. What a bitch!» Fiona said, half admiringly. She looked around: «Where are we now, by the way?»

«Das ist ein Trockendock. Hier können große Schiffe repariert werden», erklärte Edzard, «in den letzten Jahren ist hier allerdings nicht mehr viel los.»

«And how do we get away? Will the police pick us up or do we have to hitch a lift from a *Hafenrundfahrtsboot*?»

Edzard schien ihre Frage nicht wahrgenommen zu haben. «Hey, do you know something? You look really gorgeous with wet hair and wet clothes», he said looking admiringly at Fiona.

«Vorsicht», she replied, «ein guter Detektiv bleibt immer ein lonesome cowboy, as we say in English.» When she saw his disappointed look she put her arm around his shoulder and said: «Do you know what we can do once this is all over and we've talked to my father and found out the details from the police?»

«Du lernst Matjes essen!»

«God, no! But we could do with a really boring holiday. Plenty of sight-seeing and things like that.»

«O ja, Wattwanderung, Deich, nochmal Störtebeker und natürlich die Fischerboote von Greetsiel!»

«Edzard! You and your fish! One of these days you'll turn into one. I'm sure you'd make a good fish», she laughed and pushed him backwards into the water. Im Fallen griff er ihre Hand und zog sie ebenfalls ins Wasser.

«Just you wait, you cheeky little missy», prustete er, «das sag ich Dolly!»

Foto: Peer Koopmann

roro
ro

rotfuchs

«I like reading – und du?»
Deutsch-englische Geschichten von Emer O'Sullivan und Dietmar Rösler

Butler & Graf
Ein deutsch-englischer Krimi
3-499-20480-0

**Butler, Graf & Friends:
Nur ein Spiel?**
Ein deutsch-englischer Krimi
3-499-20531-9

**Butler, Graf & Friends:
Umwege**
Ein deutsch-englischer Krimi
3-499-20647-1

It could be worse – oder?
Eine deutsch-englische Geschichte
3-499-20374-X

Mensch, be careful!
Eine deutsch-englische Geschichte
3-499-20417-7

I like you – und du?
Eine deutsch-englische Geschichte
Paddy zieht mit seiner Mutter nach Berlin und geht mit Karin eine etwas komplizierte Freundschaft ein. Er spricht kaum Deutsch, und Karin kann schlecht Englisch. Sie unterhalten sich in einem witzigen Sprachmischmasch, der es ermöglicht, den ganzen Text ohne Wörterbuch aus dem Inhalt heraus zu verstehen. Am Ende haben die Leser mehr gelernt als in manchen mühsamen Lektionen in der Schule.

Emer O'Sullivan
Dietmar Rösler
**I like you –
und du?**

rororo

3-499-20323-5

Foto: Michael Nischke/Bavaria

rororo Rotfuchs

Spannende Bücher zu jungen Lebenswelten in unserer Zeit

**Frederik Hetmann/
Harald Tondern
Die Nacht, die kein Ende nahm**
In der Gewalt von Skins
3-499-20747-8

**Anatol Feid/Natascha Wegner
Trotzdem hab ich meine Träume**
*Die Geschichte von einer,
die leben will*
3-499-20552-1

**Heide Hassenmüller
Gute Nacht, Zuckerpüppchen**
3-499-20614-5

**Frauke Kühn
Das Mädchen am Fenster**
3-499-21167-X

**Margret Steenfatt
Hass im Herzen**
Im Sog der Gang
3-499-20648-X

**Harald Tondern
Wehe, du sagst was!**
Die Mädchengang von St. Pauli
3-499-20995-0

**Ann Ladiges
«Hau ab, du Flasche!»**
Immer häufiger greift Roland zur Flasche, wenn es Probleme gibt. Lange merken die Eltern nicht, wie abhängig er ist. Bis zu dem Tag, als er den Ring seiner Mutter versetzt. Kann Roland sich jetzt noch selber «aufs Trockene» retten?

3-499-20178-X